Mind Travel

ROCKY EARL SMITH

authorHOUSE®

AuthorHouse™
1663 Liberty Drive
Bloomington, IN 47403
www.authorhouse.com
Phone: 1 (800) 839-8640

This is a work of fiction. All of the characters, names, incidents, organizations, and dialogue in this novel are either the products of the author's imagination or are used fictitiously.

Published by AuthorHouse   11/09/2015

ISBN: 978-1-5049-6001-4 (sc)
ISBN: 978-1-5049-6000-7 (e)

Print information available on the last page.

Any people depicted in stock imagery provided by Thinkstock are models, and such images are being used for illustrative purposes only. Certain stock imagery © Thinkstock.

This book is printed on acid-free paper.

Because of the dynamic nature of the Internet, any web addresses or links contained in this book may have changed since publication and may no longer be valid. The views expressed in this work are solely those of the author and do not necessarily reflect the views of the publisher, and the publisher hereby disclaims any responsibility for them.

Contents

Introduction vii

Author's notes xi

Thoughts from Darkbrain xiii

The Necromancer, the story of the powerful wizard Dazzle 1

Making Changes Better 16

Death Riches 17

Completion 40

Assorted Inputs 41

Dispute This 41

The Multidimensional Elevators 43

My Dreams 53

The World Within the World 54

King Satan 64

The Rollercoaster Ride to the Unknown 76

The Spirit of Life 86

The Unlimited Mind 88

The Legend of the Ice Cream Vendor Murders 89

I Must Prevail 108

I, Fantasy 109

The Rainbow Illusion 110

I Am Vapor, Master of The Rainbow
and Keeper of the Pot of Gold 111

True Freedom 124

Introduction

I see the universe as it unfold turning zero velocity into existence, I see the wonders of matter and gravity joining forces creating mind boggling sights of pure majestic grandeur. Galaxies upon galaxies, high powered exploding novas, deep dark holes in an infinite space in which nothing escapes, small specks of dust forming life galore, I see life I see death, I see sickness I see death, I see tragedy I see death, my mind see it all, my mind explore it all, my mind experience it all and then my mind record it all, it's an amazing journey when my Mind Travel.

Mind Travel my second book possessing a series of short adventures that engages all of the mind's assets, from one extreme unto the other all levels of the mind seek entertainment, be it meditation or fantasy, psycho trophic or technology the mind hinges on avoiding boredom. Which is one reason why the power of the mind is awesome think I mean really think wow what a rush, these latest trips of terror will grasp your thoughts with rush after rush of intoxicating euphoria, you will get drunk on anticipation, high on exhilaration, which will cause a hangover of expectations, nuff said Read.

The Necromancer the story of the powerful wizard Dazzle

'Hear me all wind of the atmospheric hemisphere I command you to full power take shape of catastrophic tornadoes and level this entire region, let nothing withstand this onslaught,' shouted the power wizard and the winds did as commanded

Author's notes

Greetings I am Darkbrain-master of delusional tales of terror, my eyes see nothing but dark space as I look upon the state of existence, space deprived of decency, space without any moral substance, dark space full of evil, full of treachery, full of deceit. As my vision penetrate deeper into the dark unknown I see scenarios of nightmarish proportions, scenarios that come straight from the pits of the abyss, terror that sends chills of devastating horror through my relentless dark brainwaves. These are the horrific truths that inspire my writings, the mystery of man's mind and how his deeds are shaped directly from the evil that oozes from his uncanny thoughts, I write exactly what I see in the dark realms of reality, so get ready, you are about to connect with a brainwave that's going to leave you in a state of emotional uncertainty, utter bewilderment, and total confusion, I Darkbrain am about to share what truly is unparalleled tales of terror.

Thoughts from Darkbrain

We are so quick to judge others when we see fault in them, now think for a moment, look deep into your mind, your deep down thoughts, can you see clearly into your innermost feelings, your true being, what do you see when you get past the light that shines so brilliantly in your everyday thoughts, what lies beyond that level, yes I'm talking about that lower level, the one that explores the subconscious, the you without the masquerade, the you without resistance, the you that's kept down on that lower level for a legitimate reason, the you that caused humanity to fall from grace, look at that entity for a moment, can you see into your true self, now do you still think you have the right to judge anyone

The Necromancer, the story of the powerful wizard Dazzle

'Hear me winds of the atmospheric hemisphere as I command you to full power, take shape of catastrophic tornadoes and level this entire region, let nothing withstand this onslaught' shouted the powerful wizard and the winds did as commanded the violent attack left nothing recognizable. The wizard looked around and laugh eeriely once admiring his handy work his wrath succeeded and he vanished, years passed but the history books labeled it as one of the worst natural disaster ever recorded an entire country laid in ruins no living creature survived. Not many people living today was around during that horrific event but those that were will never forget hearing the news flash and the millions of people that died not in a day but in a matter of seconds, never before or since has nature displayed such fury and people can only pray that it never happens again. But the practice of necromancy had began to grow in every part of this now world more and more people believe that they could not only communicate with the spirits of the dead but that those spirits were a big influence in their everyday lives, in fact some consulted the spirits from the beginning of their day until they closed their eyes to sleep. Some used those spirits against living foes seeking vengeance they were of course labeled witches or warlocks, all of them displayed enormous power, but Dazzle excelled in the art of mastering the spirits his influence captured not only the spirits will but their unequaled loyalty, Dazzle became so powerful that the winds the seas the earth itself would open at his command, yes all of the elements were his to command. But what made him so dangerous was that he was a very selfish wizard with very spoil tendencies and because he was having a bad day he destroyed that country

Yes the dude would destroy entire countries killing millions of people just because he was having a bad day, all witches and warlocks feared Dazzle so all would accommodate his every command. Dazzle would for his own amusement caused great whirlwinds form level five hurricanes, command oceans to completely engulf huge continents, life meant nothing to him, no one's nor nothing's, because they were all more valuable to him dead in that state he could ruled them because their free will would die with them so then they were loyal to a fault. But there's always going to be opposition and this opposition came in the form of a God, the god Substance had viewed Dazzle's actions with disgust vowing to put an end to his madness and as the powerful wizard was in the act of his latest catastrophe summoning the seas to form a whirlpool to sink a large vacationing cruise ship the god Substance descended in a flash of thunderous power and stood in the midst of the ensuing whirlpool catching the wizard Dazzle completely

By surprise never before had his power been challenged never before had anyone or anything dared to oppose his will, who was this the god Substance was an unfamiliar form and needless to say an unwelcome presence,' who are you' shouted Dazzle 'I am Substance the god of matter and you are in violation this madness must stop at once, 'the god replied' your actions are punitive you're not at liberty to perform such autocracy cease this behavior at once or prepare for battle,' but this only angered the powerful wizard' Substance be warned my power is unmatched do not invite my wrath against you be gone at once,' the wizard demanded the wizard had never before had a justifiable reason to cause such despicable destruction even though he had become accustomed to it but now in his angered state of mind he not only had a reason but a directive and the wizard acted accordingly, directing his power and anger toward the god. The elements took on a rage the atmosphere had never encountered, wave after wave of wind, water, electrical fire, molten heat pounded the god shaking the planet to it's very core, the god had never saw the wizard in this catastrophic mode it was if he sought to destroy all life and as if on cue the spirits of the dead rose up in allegiance and awaited the wizard's command. The god, Substance looked at the steady insurmountable multiplying of the spirits of the dead as the wizard claimed more and more lives and knew this would be the battle of his life so far, although he had seen the wizard in action previously he had no idea that his newly found enemy was this powerful

It was as if he commanded existence itself, which left the god wondering if he could overcome such extreme might, but still he had to try he could not allow the wizard to proceed without challenge he knew without a doubt that that was not an option, so with no thought for his own safety the god of matter displayed his own powers beginning with taking the power to command matter away from the wizard limiting him to commanding the spirits of the dead only, but that power alone carried substantial weight because the spirits of the dead were not actual matter the god of matter found himself in unfamiliar chaos and the wizard took full advantage of the situation by commanding the spirits to attack the god in unrelentless drives so much so that the god found himself severely outnumbered and overpowered which in turn left him no other choice but to retreat and seek other methods of help. Once the wizard saw the god retreating he summoned all of the spirits of the dead and ordered them back to their resting places to remain until he sent for them again and at his command the spirits resumed their rest, then Dazzle vanished knowing that this wasn't going to be his last encounter with the god Substance and knowing also that when the god did return his powers would somehow be greater, but the wizard was confident that just like this encounter he would be the victor of every battle, but he had no doubt that the god would be a nuisance. Never before had anyone or anything challenged his authority and now an unknown god dared, so the powerful wizard Dazzle contemplated their next meeting, a meeting he was sure would be their last. Years passed before the wizard's next appearance, fresh and more powerful than ever Dazzle lashed out, his fury reaching the entire planet in record time, it was like the earth had been possessed nothing remained in any form of normalcy the elements were under his total command and all of the spirits of the dead which had grown significantly since he last summoned them were gathered for battle. The wizard had thought long and hard about the god Substance interference and had returned with a vengeance, he wasn't going to let up he would continue to pound the earth with catastrophic destruction until the god came to stop him, so the onslaught continued with thousands dying by the second which in turn caused the spirits of the dead to mount to an alarming pace. The wizard's power was defying even the laws of gravity, causing his form to reach zero gravity at which point

The wizard elevated becoming a unrestricted form, free to roam the skies at will and roam he did overseeing the destruction his powerful form was orchestrating, he felt invincible totally indestructible, he felt he was the most powerful force in the universe and as if on cue the god Substance appeared in the midst of the calamity and without hesitation the powerful wizard Dazzle commanded the overwhelming army of the spirits of the dead to attack the god and attack they did with skilled precedence the god stopped the wizard's control over matter as he had done in their previous battle the elements calmed instantly the destruction to life on earth was enormous, Substance knew he could never allow the wizard to regain any amount of control over the elements again, but he would have to figure that out later because right now these spirits, these many spirits was causing great harm to his person and he began to wonder what had happened to his newly formed ally, Destitute the goddess of the dead, she had been assigned to help him defeat these powerful spirits by Destine, the god of destiny and so far she was a no show causing Substance to suffer immensely at the hands

Of the spirits and then she was there in the midst of the chaos smiling fiendishly, looking at her smile made Substance very happy that she was on his side and when her smile stopped the spirits of the dead stopped as well, it was as if they had all fallen into a deep hypnotic trance, they were all immobile staring into space itself and then as if on cue even though the goddess didn't utter a single word all of the spirits looked toward Destitute as she vanished and with her they also vanished leaving the powerful wizard facing an angry god. Now the war's outcome would be decided between the two powerful figures without the added evil troops, Substance the all powerful god of matter itself and Dazzle the master of black magic and as the two of them sized each other up a great calm came over the whole planet, the atmosphere itself was totally silent, no form of life dared to stage any resistance nor utter any sound whatsoever, it was like the earth itself had stopped rotating on it's axis all in anticipation of the mega event about to take place. With Substance thinking that he finally had the wizard where he wanted him he struck first and merciless but Dazzle stood completely confused, never before had he faced a foe without his most dominating powers, and this baffled him to the point of exhaustion, he no longer wanted this fight, he felt he had unfairly been stripped of his defenses and left totally vulnerable before a powerful god fighting with a vengeance, a vengeance the wizard was beginning to feel in maximum volume and since the wizard was no fool he reasoned that his only recourse was to retreat and live to fight another day, so he vanished because he desperately needed time to regroup, time to come up with a viable plan, a plan to prevent his demise. The god Substance was angered beyond control he was so close to victory that he could sense it, he tried unsuccessfully to discern any remnant of the wizard but no matter of him was left so the god took control of his persona even though he knew it could be centuries until the wizard's next appearance

The god knew he had no choice but to wait and Substance also knew that Dazzle's next appearance would be more sinister and devious than any of his previous ones so he had to be prepared for any scenario the wizard could conjure up so the god hesitively vanished as well. But the god's frustration mounted so much so that he found it impossible to just wait for the wizard to decide their next meeting so Substance began seeking help from other gods. His first stop was with the god of darkness Midnight, Substance tried hard to convince the god of darkness that the wizard was not only a threat to life itself but that he seek to overthrow the gods themselves because he reasoned that if anyone could find the wizard's lair the god of darkness would be the one. But Midnight declined to help because he was quite fun of the wizard and chose not to stop his folly, but vowed not to help him either, so Substance next stop was with Nimbus the god of light, surely this god would join his plight in ending the wizard's reign of terror and Substance was not disappointed, the god of light agreed that Dazzle's treachery must end at once and together but cautiously they approached Destitute the goddess of the dead to be reassured that she was still an ally and she agreed not because she cared one way or the other about the wizard's actions, her gripe was that he used her domain with no regard to her authority. So the three gods formed an allegiance with one express purpose the total destruction of the powerful wizard Dazzle, Substance would use his power over all matter to seek his whereabouts, Nimbus the god of light would search all of darkness seeking the wizard's lair and Destitute the goddess of the dead would send the spirits into every part of their existing domain with strict orders to report any sightings, feelings or anything remotely familiar to the great wizard. Time passed with no results until the spirits found his lair and wasted no time alerting the goddess of their finding, and the goddess wicked smile returned to her face, a smile so fiendish that the other two gods were glad she was their ally and not their enemy, then Destitute revealed all to her allies and together as planned beforehand the three of them went into action, operation destroy the wizard and as they converged on his lair each of them saw a scenario but neither of them realized it. The great wizard had anticipated such a move and had taken great steps in preparing for the occasion, he knew from their last encounter the only way possible for him to assure victory was to bring his enemies here to his world where he commanded all, so he allowed the spirits to discern his whereabouts knowing they would lead his enemies here for their final showdown, and now after seeing his plan in full effect Dazzle's confidence grew, so much so that he smiled

An unfamiliar command of his facial muscles because the wizard hadn't smile in centuries, his bitterness had seen to that but now he brandish a smile of pure confidence. The stage was set and the mighty wizard began his attack catching the gods by surprise, the three hadn't saw this coming because they thought they had the advantage so none of them was quite ready for the wizard's onslaught but they knew instantly that they had seriously underestimated this evil being so it took them awhile to figure out a counterattack because of the fact that they each encountered a different scenario. Substance the god of matter faced antimatter which proved to be a worthy foe pretty much nullifying his powers to the point of serious frustration and Substance cursed the day the wizard came to be. Nimbus the god of light encountered the darkest radiation in the universe and then the two gods were combated by dark matter it was all they could do not to retreat they both knew the wizard had great powers but they had no idea he could reach out and grab all the powers of the universe which his previous encounter with zero gravity bestowed upon him so the two gods knew one thing for sure, Dazzle could not be allowed to survive this battle he was too dangerous, too powerful. Destitute the goddess of the dead had to be dealt with in a totally different manner, since matter had no power over her domain the great wizard had to come up with a plan that exceeded all others and it had to include spirits, spirits that had never had the chance to possess a body therefore wasn't in the goddess command, and as these spirits emerged so did the goddess spirits of the dead until their numbers exceeded accountability and once the great wizard saw the scene before him he smiled once more and gave the order to attack. Destitute looked puzzled, never before had she encountered spirits that wasn't hers to command so this scenario took her completely by surprise, so far Dazzle's plan was going perfect just as he had foreseen it, the spirits wasted no time attacking the goddess and her multitude of followers, meanwhile Substance powers being nullified by antimatter and dark matter left him helpless so as furious as he was he had no recourse but to retreat and try to find another way to combat the wizard which was pretty much the same setting for Nimbus because of all of dark radiation the wizard had employed from the depths of the universe. And now with two of his enemies out of the way Dazzle could focus solely on the one remaining Destitute the goddess of the dead but once returning his attention back to this battle the wizard noticed his army of spirits declining at a very rapid rate and this puzzled him because he had done his homework and knew without a doubt that these spirits were just as powerful as the spirits of the dead, so what was happening, why was his army of spirits being defeated, how could this be possible and with that he turned his attention to Destitute herself to find the answers

And it didn't take the wizard long to see why he was losing the battle, the goddess had grown to an alarming height and it didn't appear she would be stopping anytime soon because as more of the wizard's spirit filled army vanquished the more height was added to the goddess statue and soon Destitute stood larger than life, even by the standards of a god's life and as she looked around the wizard's lair it soon became apparent that she enjoyed her new statue and she acknowledged it with her now familiar fiendish smile and then at her command her spirits attacked the wizard and Dazzle fought back, he now had powers great enough to defeat gods so he called on the powers of the universe itself, but there was no stopping the goddess onslaught she had become too powerful and it flowed down into her spirits so much so that the wizard started to succumb, usually at this point the wizard vanishes, retreating to his lair to regroup, but this time that wasn't an option because the goddess was destroying his lair with a vengeance, the wizard confused and badly beaten sought to just vanish anyway, even though his lair was being completely destroyed there had to be a place, somewhere that he could seek refuge because at this rate he knew it wouldn't be long before his demise became the goddess trophy. So he vanished at least he tried to but somehow in his present condition his powers were hard to control and he couldn't help noticing that the goddess was reaching down seemingly to finish what no one during all of these centuries had been able to accomplish and for the first time since Dazzle became the powerful wizard he knew fear, the two gods Substance and Nimbus had returned to the wizard's lair to somehow help their ally but after observing the direction the battle had taken both breathe a sigh of relief and they also had the same thought after again witnessing the goddess fiendish smile and that was that they were glad to be her allies instead of enemies. But Dazzle wasn't just going to lay down and die as he was proving by casting every form of magic that he still possess at the goddess as she kneeled down to finish him off and though his remaining powers were awesome Destitute was relentless, and true enough the wizard's desperate attempt at survival had a traumatic effect on the goddess persons but she refused to succumb and continued her assault and then she had the wizard in her grasp lifting him as he kicked and punched, demanding to be released and of course his demands were fruitless as she continued to raise him higher and higher until she figured that the level was sufficient enough to end the wizard's reign of terror permanently and then without hesitation she flung him toward the waiting ground below and as she and her two allies watched in anticipation gravity pulled the powerful wizard toward his death, but all of the gods had forgotten that Dazzle had the power to defy gravity and defy it he did and now he had also recovered enough to vanish and with much disappointment the three deities watch as the wizard became intangible. Destitute's fiendish smile became unparalleled anger as she let out a deaf defying scream that shook her very surroundings, Substance started weeping all the while cursing the day he had encountered the wizard and Nimbus just stood there in complete and utter shock, total disbelief, how could this have happened, what is it going to take to rid the world of this evil destroyer and all three gods in anger returned to their perspective lair's to come up with a plan to annuilate

The wizard for good and it was no doubt in any of their minds that they would need additional help to fulfill their quest, they had all underestimated the sinister mind of the great wizard a mistake they each vowed wouldn't happen again, so the next plan of action would have to be flawless, at all cost the wizard had to die. But the wizard was no fool either, he knew now that he was vulnerable and he realized as well that the gods were not stupid and that the next battle between them would surely be the last, so he had to pull out all stops and seek allies to enhance his chances, allies that was as ruthless as he was and had the power to match. He reasoned that the gods would also incorporate help and there was no doubt in his mind that the next meeting between his forces and their's would shake the very foundations of the universe itself and put an end to this war. The wizard was tired, not the normal weariness that he usually felt when he could go to his lair and regroup, no this went way beyond that, the exhaust he felt now level his very being in all phases driving the point deeper and deeper that he couldn't survive another attack of this magnitude and for a brief moment Dazzle's mind flashed back to the time of the goddess reaching down and grabbing him and the fear that he felt at that moment, she had him and she could have easily ended his life right then and there but thankfully for him that she had chosen the wrong method of carrying out that sentence and that had allowed him to regain his composure and live to fight another day, a day when he would make them all pay. But trying to think of entities he could incorporate was no easy task, sure he knew of some that was just as devious as he was but none that wanted to battle the gods, in fact the ones he wanted to join forces with were gods, really who is better qualified to battle gods than other gods. So the

The powerful wizard began working on a spell, a delusion if you will that would allow him to take control of the minds of gods, he knew that if he accomplished this feat it would be his masterpiece, it wasn't going to be easy but he knew that if it could be done he was the one who could do it, and then a much more sobering thought overtook him and that was that he had no other options this spell success or failure would seal his fate. So he cross incantations that were proven with others that had not yet been employed, tirelessly he worked from day one leaving no spell untried whether it dealt with controlling the mind or not he reasoned that in this long list of delusional incantations there had to be at least one that would assist him in fulfilling his mission, so he pushed himself on and on refusing to take the break his being so desperately needed until finally he was sure he had the delusion required, but of course until the spell was actually cast there was always room for error, but nonetheless phase one of his plan was accomplished and now to phase two, employing allies that possess the power and motive to fight the battle at hand. So Dazzle set his mind to thinking, going back to the time he first became the great wizard until now, remembering every foe he had come up against, remembering all the bystanders that had actually enjoyed the display of power he had brandished in his many disasters and the one that stood out the most was Midnight the god of darkness, he had observed the god admiring his handy work on more than one occasion which led the wizard to believe that he could persuade him to join him in his plight, but to the wizard's disappointment the god of darkness declined. The wizard's concentration intensified who could he possibly ask next, and then Combustible the god of fire entered his mind,

A god that had also admired his work on more than one occasion, but Combustible also declined, what is it with these gods thought the wizard, he knew that secretly they longed to be menaces while outwardly they upheld certain godly standards but regardless of their reasoning Dazzle still found himself alone in his quest and this troubled him because how could he possibly hope to control the minds of gods he was at war with when he couldn't even persuade gods whom he had no quarrel with and then it dawned on him, the incantation, the mind controlling spell he had brewed in his quest to win the war, it had to be the answer, this would be the perfect test, he would use it to persuade the gods that had denied him allegiance and if it proved successful then he felt victory was assured. Brilliant thought the wizard as he set out to revisit the gods of his choosing, the god of darkness Midnight watched Dazzle as he approached wondering what diabolical scheme the wizard did concoct since his last visit and knowing to be vigilant himself because he rejected the wizard's request, after observing the wizard over the centuries he knew that rejection was not an option in his mind and as the wizard approached he noticed the alarm on the god's face which enhanced his already awareness that his plan had to be flawless, there was no room at all for mistakes, 'Join my mind with the god of darkness, his control is what I seek, let my will overtake his whole being and let that change be swift and complete' and once the wizard had spoken these words his powerful magic filled the air, bombarding Midnight's mind with wave after wave of hypnotic incantational might until the expression on the god's face completely change, a totally blank stare replaced the very confident one and the wizard knew that the spell was a success. And now he directed Midnight to follow his lead and soon they were face to face with Combustible, the god of fire,

It didn't surprise the god to see the wizard' s soon return in fact from what he had observed over the centuries him not returning would have been a surprise, but seeing the god of darkness accompany him sent out some warning signs in his mind, a very likely pair but an uncanny allegiance thought Combustible but before the god could respond to misfits the wizard cast his magic into the air,' join my mind with the god of fire his control is what I seek, let my will overtake his being and let that change be swift and complete,' and to the wizard's satisfaction the incantation worked on Combustible as well, now Dazzle's confidence was growing he was beginning to feel like his former self again, invincible because now he reasoned that the war would be won without physical confrontation instead by his hypnotic magical delusions and so feeling all powerful again he directed the two gods to follow him. The next stop was the lair of Nimbus the god of light, the god couldn't believe his eyes, the enemy had come to him and with two powerful yet unlikely allies and of course this puzzled the god alone with giving him a very uneasy feeling, he liked his chances battling the wizard but with two powerful gods at his side Combustible could only think of trying to summon his allies, but before the god could react Dazzle cast his magic into the air and now the wizard's allies stood at three with Substance the god of matter on his radar. The wizard felt more powerful than he ever could have imagined he was commanding gods and he couldn't help but think that he should have thought of this long ago it would have saved him a lot of pain and anguish, but now as he thought of the source in which the pain originated the wizard smiled as they approached the lair of Substance the god of matter, this would be the sweetest victory so far and sure enough when Substance saw Dazzle and the three gods at his side especially Nimbus his most trusted ally, the god of matter became panic stricken knowing something was terribly wrong and his first instinct was to flee and get help from Destitute the goddess of the dead, but that one moment of indecision proved tragic, because that little time was all the wizard needed to cast his mind controlling spell and he didn't hesitate, the god of matter never knew what hit him and now the wizard's allies became four with one adversary remaining Destitute the goddess of the dead herself, once she was in his control Dazzle knew he could resume his catastrophic ways with no resistance, this though not only made the wizard smile but laugh out loud and laugh he did and noticed all of his allies was laughing as well and the laughing stop as they approached the lair of Destitute

And yes the goddess was aware of their presence and the wizard was relieved to see that she wasn't the giant figure he had encountered during their last conflict, but still she sent an aura of dominance like no other deity the wizard had ever fought against and for some reason even with all of his allies at his side Dazzle's confidence was still shaken to the point that his hands began shaking and his mind knew mass confusion, but the great wizard knew he had to overcome this temporary lapse, he knew he had to regain his composure for his spell to work, so he focused his total concentration and full power into the incantation as he uttered the words once more,' join my mind with the goddess of the dead her control is what I seek, let my will overtake her whole being and let that change be swift and complete,' and as the wizard finished his incantation he looked at the goddess in anticipation of dominating her in every way after all she nearly killed him so yes this victory would be his greatest, but something went wrong, he noticed as he looked into her eyes, there was no blank stare in fact he had never seen eyes with more control, more confidence fear took the wizard's mind, his body, every fiber of his being and paralyzed them, but somehow his four allies came to his thoughts and calmed him somewhat, they were his only hope so he pulled himself together enough to turn toward them shouting commands, but none of the gods responded and that's it dawned on the wizard that his allies were no longer under his control but under the goddess, the incantation that had flowed from the wizard's mouth into Destitute's mind had somehow had a ricocheting effect causing the hypnotic waves to backfire giving her control over all of the minds that were in his command and now the goddess realizing what had happen displayed her now infamous fiendish smile, a smile that shook the core of all who witnessed it. The wizard was furious his fear had completely subsided he had somehow fallen under Destitute's control as well, his conscious mind was enslaved but his subconscious fought the controlling signals echoing from her psychic but when the goddess sensed his inner resistance

She willed her remaining four allies to destroy the wizard with every weapon at their command and even though the gods didn't quite understand why the order was uttered they still responded without hesitation and Dazzle felt the full fury of his once allies now enemies as each one of them pounded him with blow after earth shattering blow sending him into total confusion thus rendering him completely defenseless, the goddess was content to just watch the utter destruction of her once formidable foe, the great wizard had chose to use his most powerful asset, his mastery of magic in his quest to rule all without resistance and it almost worked to perfection, but the mistake he made was underestimating the mind of Destitute the goddess of the dead and it became a fatal mistake, because of the fact that her mind doesn't operate like other minds, her mind is unique, loyal to no one or nothing, the only reason she had joined forces with the other gods is because the wizard had impeded his will on her loyal subjects the spirits of the dead and that had pissed her off, but she was loyal to herself only, therefore no magical spell or incantation could control a mind with no emotions, no feelings whatsoever, no power can control a mind that's cold as ice, which is why the powerful wizard's mind fought against the goddess will because the wizard himself was loyal to himself only and in the end it rendered his spirit helpless. He still roam the universe making an appearance every few centuries but his powers have been completely nullified, no longer can his presence upset the flow of anything, matter is now completely controlled by Substance the god of matter, all dark radiation is controlled by Midnight the god of darkness, light is back in total control of Nimbus the god of light, and all heat is controlled again by Combustible the god of fire in fact none of the gods ever had a problem with their powers being infringed on thanks to Destitute the goddess of the dead and now queen of the gods.

Making Changes Better

-written by \Rocky Earl Smith

So much darkness I get chills, so much light it's soothing to feel

So much evil running rapid, so much good it becomes a habit

So many changes it boggles the mind, so much routine it drags the time

So much energy it rivals expectations, so much negativity it brings on depression

Keeping up with the pace, never losing my grace

With exquisite good taste, I can win this race. Peace

Death Riches

written by Rocky Earl Smith- a.k.a Dark Brain

'Clarence let us in we need to use the restroom' I said as I continued to beat on the front door,' he's in there I can see him moving around', but before I could complete my sentence Mark started knocking profusely on the front window,' let us in man', he shouted but still no answer came from within, this was highly unusual him ignoring us this way, then I stopped knocking because a very disturbing feeling overshadowed me but Mark continued to beat on the window. Just about that time Clarence came out of the house onto the front porch and faced Mark with a pistol in his hand which upon seeing I back off of the porch hoping that this was all a nightmare, but as I watched Clarence pointed the gun directly at the concrete firing once and then a second boom was heard before he raised it and aim directly at Mark's abdomen and fired a third shot and as I looked in horror for a short time both men just stood there as if in shock and then Mark raised his hands and clutched his abdomen sinking to the porch in agonizing pain and then he was gone, after seeing what had just transpired I ran back to the car and put it in reverse then once I was completely out of Clarence sight I called for help, but strange as it was the number I dialed was not for the emergency personnel, but to our mother but I couldn't complete the call because for some reason my cell phone was not push button but rotary which made dialing any alignment of numbers impossible while in motion, so I hit the brakes and once the car had stopped for some reason I still couldn't complete the dialing process and now feeling trapped in a dire predicament with no recourse I decided to pull the car forward just enough to see what was happening on that porch. What was Clarence doing now that he had killed my brother, his nephew, and as I proceeded past the wood fence that separates the two yards I glanced toward the crime scene which is now my brother's deathbed and was stunned to see my brother Mark sitting upright in a hearse but staring mindlessly ahead as the driver backed out of the driveway, as I looked closer at my brother's face he looked alive even with that blank stare and then I caught a glimpse of the driver of the hearse and yes it was Clarence also having a blank stare in his eyes and that's when I awoke sweating profusely, my head pounding like a sonic boom had traveled through my brains, I sat up trying to grasp reality, this recurring nightmare was driving me insane, I was losing all sense of reality, why did I keep having this unspeakable dream, it made no sense whatsoever because my brother Mark and my uncle Clarence died years ago so what was the meaning of this torture or was some evil spirit tormenting me. I got out of bed and got lost in the shower, this had become the normal procedure after the recurring epic, the water was still soothing but it was beginning to lose it's magic, I've got to find a way to end this madness or I felt I would be joining them very soon, but as hard as I tried looking at it from every angle it still made no sense and needless to say sleep was not an option for the remaining hours of that night. I sat on my porch and tried to count every star in the night sky, the moon was only half full as it sat in the heavens staring back at me, but even with the full serenity of the heavens in full view of my eyes, my mind was in limbo, halfway between reality and insanity, the view of my brother being murdered by my uncle clouded my thoughts, suffocating any logic that dared to enter, I can still see the pain on my brother's face as he clutched his stomach and fell to the pavement his eyes becoming a blank stare as the life exit his body and the anger on my uncle's face becoming a blank stare as well, the rotary dial cell phone, the unsuccessful call for help and why was I attempting to call our mother first instead of the emergency respondent needed to handle such a dire situation, it was about that time that I felt a warming caressing sensation on my face, my body, captivating my mind so much that reality took charge of my life again and I found myself staring straight into the sun's ultraviolet rays which now occupied the space that the moon previously had, I was exhausted, I wanted to call and tell my secretary to cancel all of today's activities and inform the answering service to monitor all calls and then take the day off, but then why sat here and wallow in this stupid surreal puzzle, no I think it would do my mind better to go about my normal workday and hope upon hope that I never have that nightmare again. The thought sounded good but I found myself sitting in my office staring deep into my P.C. screen in a complete daze,' Luke', I heard someone repeating my name as my unwelcome thoughts were interrupted, I looked up to see my secretary looking at me inquizable, 'Luke, Ms. Patricia Anderson is waiting in the reception room', she informed me,' uh oh yeah, send her in,' I managed to say though still in a state of confusion from the hypnotic scenes going through my head, but about that time I heard my secretary tell Patricia she could enter my office. Patricia was a potential new client who seemed to know her way around according to our correspondence by email, but I base my opinions on personal gatherings, I think a person's body language and facial expression say a lot more about them than their entertaining words, but as she entered my office I was somewhat surprise by her sheer beauty, the shapely build of her body was very transparent even though she dress professionally 'mr. Rich, Luke Rich,' Patricia acknowledge, 'yes and you are Patricia Anderson, I'm glad we meet formally at last won't you be seated' I replied,' Thank you Mr Rich as I corresponded with you on email I pretty much sum the whole business experience up except for a few minor details, one of which being that in a business relationship there are no certified hours of operation from my point of view complete flexibility is one of the major keys to success and the other I feel I have to mention because of the way you looked at me when I entered your office is that I don't date business partners again from my experience is a recipe for failure and in our line of business failure is not an option', she completed' Ms Anderson I totally agree, now to the business at hand and of course there will be a lot of traveling involved', I said,' of course' she agreed,' then I see no reason why we can't have the contracts drawn up at once and if satisfactory to us both we'll sign and put success in motion', I stated' Mr Rich you're my kind of partner I really feel good about this,' Patricia stated' Renee' I summoned my secretary,' have our lawyers contact Ms Anderson's lawyers with the agreement I'm sending you via email and label it urgent',' I'm on it Luke' my secretary informed me,' Ms Anderson you'll have the contract by day's end and as for the flexible hours you can choose to start today or fresh in the morning I'll leave that to your discretion', I informed her, she stood to her feet as did I and extended her hand which of course I immediately shook as a form of sealing the deal,' I'd like to celebrate our new partnership over dinner I'm buying, you choose the restaurant,' she said' how can I refuse such a grateful offer I'll be delighted', I accepted' good' she continued,' let's make it around seven this evening shall I pick you up or do you prefer to meet at the restaurant', 'I'll meet you there' I told her' and what is the restaurant of your choice' she ask 'Confucius' I said' a very wise choice the service is exquisite I see you not only have good taste in women but you know good food as well,' she complimented me,' thank you until seven' I said' until seven' she said as she left and of course my eyes followed every step she made until she was out of my sight and then even though my eyes could no longer see her she was permanently embedded in every area of my mind, and my mind was grateful for the much needed break after the previous night of confusion that had succeeded so many nights of utter continuance, Patricia provided a form of relief that changed the whole course of the day, my whole thought pattern was different the nightmare still loom in the shadows but at least now I had some form of control and it couldn't have come at a better time,'luke' my secretary's voice interrupted my chain of thoughts,' the contracts are being drawn up and should be ready for your signature in approximately an hour','thank you Renee you're a treasure' I told her then she continued' your next client should be here momentarily' I thanked her again as she was leaving my office, once she had closed the door there was an eerie silence even though I could here my secretary's voice as she spoke to someone on the phone, probably her husband, he would call her numerous times each day seemingly just to talk but I'm thinking he's checking up on her because she worked for me all alone and I imagine his imagination really run wild thinking of all the things we could be during together. Renee is hot and I've got to admit some of the outfits she wear are very revealing, outlining each curve on her well kept body but so far it's been a look but don't touch type of relationship and yes my imagination has run wild a few times itself but Renee is very valuable to me as my secretary and I don't want to ruin that bond by trying to sleep with her, I can actually trust her to take care of things when I'm away on business, that old saying that it's hard to find good help I know to be true but Renee is the exception to the rule and as she continued her conversation with her husband I began to wonder about my next client, this one was a man and according to his emails very business minded but where was he maybe he wasn't as professional as his emails suggested and that's one of the main reasons I reserve my personal opinion until after a personal interview this guy should have been here twenty minutes ago.' Renee' I called'yes' she answered' see if you can get my next client on the phone to find out why he's late' I told her' I'm on it' she responded and about a minute later' Luke' 'yes' I answered,'there was no answer'' she said' is there another number in his info. That will reach him' I ask' no that's the only one noted' she said' alright when is my next client due to arrive' I ask' two o'clock' she answered,'thank you' I said and disconnected, two o'clock I thought what in the world could I possibly do for three hours all of a sudden the sunshine Patricia had brought to the previous meeting was gone and now I sat in a dark gloomy room even though the lights were all on, three hours now echoed through my mind it seemed like a lifetime and just then Renee entered my office' we have a lot of time to kill do you want me to order lunch' she ask' yes' I said' the usual' she ask' the usual' I responded and as she left my office headed for her desk I couldn't help but notice that the dress she was wearing was unusually short today, it was a very hot day so I'm sure it was innocent but needless to say my imagination began going off the wild rector scale I had never seen that much of her legs before, they were awesome and the way the dress hug her butt as she walked out of the room stopped all thoughts not pertaining to the view that I had just witnessed, my body responded to the view and then she was back not giving me a chance to re cooperate 'Luke our lunch is on the way can we talk' she ask 'sure what's on your mind' I said trying to maintain a level speech pattern' I have to go to the ladies room I'll be right back and then we can talk during lunch' she said as she exit the office, while she was gone our lunch arrived'how's it going' I ask the delivery guy' it's going' he responded' here's your order' and after waiting for me to confirm that he'd gotten the order right he left me sitting there staring out of the window, I had seen this view from the window countless of times but for some reason this time it was different, this time I saw the view with not just my eyes but with my mind as well, I notice every detail of the other buildings in the distance to the bus stops on both sides of the street below, the scene was disturbingly vacant as I looked at a familiar car pull up and two guys got out of it and proceeded to beat on the house across the street

'let us in we need to use the bathroom' and then tel i iling the other that he see the man in there but the man inside won't come to the door, so the other man started beating on the front window asking to be let in so they could relieve themselves, finally the man came out of the house holding a pistol in his hand and upon seeing the gun the man who had previously been knocking on the front door stepped backwards while the man who had been knocking on the window stood facing the man who held the pistol and then two shots were fired at the pavement before the gun was raised and fired directly into the man's abdomen then the two just stood there for about three seconds before the man grabbed his midsection his face expressing severe pain as he began falling to the pavement with all life leaving his body as he fell, leaving only a blank lifeless stare on his face the man who had pulled the trigger brandish the same blank stare even though he was standing upright, the guy who had stepped backwards after spotting the gun was now back in the car the two men had pulled up in backing the vehicle to the yard next door trying to shield himself from the pistol toting man on the porch with the wood fence that separated the two yards all the while holding a cell phone which he was apparently having trouble using and then as if on automatic he began pulling forward toward the yard he had just left but was too late to see what had taken place, the wood fence had shielded his eyes so he didn't see the man who had been shot get up and walk to the hearse that had been parked in the driveway getting into the back of it leaving the doors open so he could ride sitting upright, he couldn't see the man who had killed him walk around to the driver's door get behind the steering wheel and proceed backing out of the driveway,'luke, luke' Renee kept calling my name and as I awoke from the deep sleep I had fallen into I notice the sweat pouring down my face and my body shaking vigorously, I was so relieved to see her, so happy she had awaken me that my first impulse was to grab her and hug her so tight that it would render her motionless, but I managed to stop myself because the last thing I wanted to do right now was something stupid. 'luke', she said once more,'yes I'm awake now I didn't get much sleep last night I must have doze off, hmm that food smell good let's eat', I managed to say but when I saw the way she was looking at me I knew she was going to want to know more,' are you alright, are you sick do you want me to call for help', Renee went on and on,' no', I interrupted 'it was just a bad dream I'm feeling better now', I told her as I was unwrapping my sandwich,'are you sure', she added' yes I'm starved let's enjoy our lunch' I tried to sound convincing so she reluctantly dropped the conversation and unwrapped her food as well remaining silent for an unusual amount of time,' hmm that restaurant really make a mean sandwich', I said breaking the silence,' they sure do it's my favorite eatery in this area', Renee said and then after the awkwardness of that moment subsided, I said' didn't you have something you wanted to talk to me about' 'yes I do' Renee said seemingly coming out of her daze,' it's my husband, his jealousy is driving me crazy, I don't know how much longer I can endure the accusations he keep insisting that something is going on between you and I, according to his insults he doesn't trust me at all',' insults' I said inquizably 'what kind of insults'' well he has this notion that from the time I come to work it's a sexual marathon happening between us, he thinks I service you breakfast, lunch and break time', she said and then added' the way he accuses me has caused our marriage to suffer, lately I don't even want him to touch me and needless to say that feeds his suspicions, Luke I love him but if this treatment persist I'm going to leave him'' do he want you to quit your job' I asked 'he does' she said' but I don't think that would solve anything because I love my job and if I have to quit because of his jealousy then I'm going to resent him for it and that's going to open up a whole new can of worms'' Renee to be honest with you you're the best secretary I've ever had and I would definitely regret losing you but I'll respect any decision you make' I told her and after we had finished our lunch Renee gathered the empty wrappings and discarded them and then she came over to me hug me and told me I was the best employer she had ever worked for, in fact she added that I was more like her friend than her boss, then she kissed me on my lips and turned and walked out and yes my eyes were observing every movement her body made as she exited, focus I kept telling myself, you've got to stay focus. I glanced at the time wow one o'clock, two hours had passed and now with my last client of today due to arrive in about an hour I decided I would regroom myself because waking up as I did earlier had taken it's toll on my hygiene so I entered my adjoining washroom and handled my business oh yeah I told myself much better. Now with only about thirty minutes left before the meeting I decided to go over every detail concerning the client that would soon become part of my reality but no sooner had I sat down to go over my notes that my secretary informed me that my two o'clock had arrived early,' give me five minutes and then send them in', I told her this was a husband and wife team and their resume was quite impressive, okay I told myself it's showtime then the door open and my secretary announced them,' 'luke this is mr. And mrs. Charlie Ferguson' 'please come in' I said,' thank you mr. Rich' mr. Ferguson said' this is my wife Ann' he continued, 'hi I'm happy to meet you both now tell me how can we help each other' I ask and as Charlie dominated the conversation I couldn't help but wonder if his wife was going to assume some responsibility in the negotiations or was she kind of a silent partner, 'and that is how we got to this point' Charlie went on and that's when his wife Ann said 'we feel like we've come as far as we can on our own and after completing our homework on you we are very impress with your credentials and think you are the perfect partner to help us go to the next level',' thank you I'm sure we can fulfill the highest level possible now tell me exactly what are your limitations in working status' I ask very seriously, and Ann continued' well since we have no children at this point our hours are very flexible and we're both go getters so success is of the uppermost concern' 'Charlie, Ann welcome aboard you've just described the perfect formula to success in this business, I'll have my lawyers draw up the contract and get with your lawyers and I'm thinking our partnership should be official by tomorrow morning' I told them' fine we're be ready' Charlie said and after shaking both of their hands the couple left and yes I couldn't stop myself from observing Ann's form as the two walked out, Charlie really had great taste in women he certainly had a prize in Ann focus I kept telling myself focus, and then my secretary entered my office' did the meeting go well'she asked 'yes I think it's been a pretty productive day' I told her'will there be anything else today' she asked' yes have my lawyers produce one more contract with instructions to be ready to sign tomorrow morning and that will complete this day, Renee you've been a great help to me since you arrived and your loyalty is unmatched but if you decide to quit to save your marriage I'll understand completely and will give you the highest reference' I assured her 'hey are you trying to get rid of me' she said jokingly with a very seductive smile' what do you think'I answered I will see you in the morning at nine o'clock and hopefully every morning we're scheduled to work until we retire''and once we retire will I get to see you still' she asked 'sure just bring your rocking chair and sat it by mine we'll still have rhythm' I said with a smile,'count on it' she said came over and hugged me and planted a kiss on my lips then turned and walked out without saying another word, not with her mouth anyway but her body language was loud and clear, focus I kept telling myself you've got to stay focus and then Patricia came to my mind the dinner at seven o'clock, I glanced at the time it was four-twenty good I thought I've got time to go home and change but all the way home I kept wondering how I was going to work with Patricia without trying to get her into my bed don't get it twisted I'm a professional so I've worked with a few very nice looking women during my career but there was an aura about this woman that penetrated my defense mechanism and made me doubt my stability and of course I wanted my cake and eat it too. Then a very eerie feeling overshadow my thought process as I pulled into the driveway to my house the memory of my reoccurring nightmare knocked the air out of my lungs and I found myself grasping for any amount of oxygen that would start my breathing function again it literary seemed like all of the air in the earth's atmosphere had dissipated I may as well been in outer space I thought I was going to die and then just like it started it stopped and air began filling my lungs again, I can breathe I kept thinking I going to live the feeling of relief was awesome there's nothing like a near death experience that make appreciation for life exquisite so as my mind began functioning normally I just sat there in my jeep staring at my house, my yard, the neighborhood everything seemed so fresh it was like looking at them for the first time. Then as I gathered my thoughts I got out of my jeep and headed toward the front door to my house all the while feeling very uneasy and dysfunctional, here I was a very successful businessman on the verge of becoming top of the line in my field of work and stuck between two totally different realities and the one I'm in at this moment threaten the foundation of the one I just left, focus I said to myself you've got to get your head out of this dream realm and finish tackling the world you and your partners are counting on, the potential degree of success that your soon to be partners bring to the table is without a doubt motivation to overcome any obstacle be it real or in my mind and with these thoughts in mind I entered my house and got ready for my date with super hot Patricia and once I had finish grooming I looked in the full length mirror making sure everything was in the right place then I glanced at the time it was six-thirty-seven, 'six-thirty-seven' I gasp 'I've got to get going' as I approached the restaurant I looked around to see if Patricia was in sight, she wasn't so after giving the valet permission to park my jeep I entered the thinking Patricia was already there waiting at the table that had been reserved for us but she wasn't so I looked at the time it was three minutes after seven maybe she was just running a little late but I decided to call her cell phone just to make sure she was okay there was no answer 'hi pat here identify yourself and I'll get back to you' her voicemail said 'hi Pat this is Luke Rich I'm here at Confucius ring me back thank you' I spoke into the receiver, time passed no return call this was very suspicious activity totally out of character of the lady I had met with that morning and after about fifth-teen I called her number again and again her voicemail answered, something was wrong I could feel it in my spirit I started to swing by her residence on my way home but I decided against it I didn't know her like that but as I drove home that eerie feeling came over me again and I knew this was going to be a long night but I went straight home anyway I figured that would be the best thing I could do I thought that if I drowned myself in my work, listen to some musical concerts, maybe some games that these activities would fulfill the night because it was one thing I was certain of and that was sleep was not going to be an option, then the thought of Patricia not showing up for our date triumph all the other mind altering delusions I had to try her cell one more time and again I got her voicemail, soon I found myself pulling into the driveway to my home spotting someone sitting on my porch it was kind of dark but I could see the form and knew it was a woman but looking around I didn't see any kind of transportation so my first thought was that it was one of my neighbors but after getting out of my jeep and walking toward her I began noticing things about her that I recognized then as she stood the surprise on my face was unmistakable 'Renee' I said as I saw she was crying'what's wrong' but she was crying so hard I couldn't understand a word coming from her mouth I approached and hugged her 'come in and tell me what happened is it your husband did he hurt you' I asked as we entered the house 'how did you get here sit down it's going to be alright' I told her but she continued to cry uncontrollably so I just sat down and held her for a while letting her get it all out and after some time had passed she started to gain some sort of control and began to tell me what had happened 'he's crazy Luke the man I married is out of his mind'' what happened'I asked 'I went home to talk things out with him and try to come up with a solution to save our marriage but once he got home he was like a madman throwing accusations to no end, belittling and degrading the whole concept of our marriage, I tried to calm him down but he demanded that I quit my job calling you my pimp saying that I not only service you but at your command I service any or all of your clients and business partners and that made me angry so I asked him if he thought that way about me then why did he marry me then he just started cursing and hitting me, Luke I can't go back there what am I going to do I'll never let him touch me again in no kind of way'and I answered 'tonight just make yourself at home right here then tomorrow we'll figure something out' it had been an very eventful day I was tired my brain was tired on the way home I was thinking of ways to fill this night thinking sleep was not an option, now sleep was a priority I was exhausted and so after showing Renee the quest room I returned to my room undressed and collapsed the last thing I remember was hearing Renee enter the bathroom before sleep cuddled me in it's arms.

'let's stop and use the restroom' John said,' we might as well I can't hold it until I get home' I said, 'I can't either' John said, and no sooner than I had stop the car John was out and running toward the front door, I wasn't far behind him as I stepped on the porch and joined in the quest to enter. I knocked on the front door as John tapped on the window,' Clarence' we both kept calling out,' I see him in there but he won't answer' I said as I noticed John peering through the window,'Clarence let us in we have to use the restroom' John scream out and just then the door opened,' Luke are you awake' Renee's voice ended the nightmare,' yes I'm awake are you feeling better' I asked 'a little bit but I'm afraid please don't make me sleep in that lonely room I'll be good' Renee pleaded, 'come here' I told her so she got into my bed and snuggled her soft warm naked body next to mine, I put my arms around her and we both fell asleep almost immediately, for some reason my sleep was very peaceful no nightmares in fact I don't remember dreaming at all. I awoke the next morning to the ringing of my phone' yes' I said' Mr. Rich this is Charlie Ferguson have you received our signed contract yet" give me one sec.' I told him as I checked my emails 'yes it's official partner we're in business' I told him 'great' he said'I will contact you as soon as your first project is ready which should be in about one hour'I told him' super we'll be ready' he said as we disconnected that worked out well I thought smiling but then Patricia entered my mind her not showing up at the restaurant for our date the previous night was very puzzling especially considering it was in celebrating our new work partnership, I couldn't help thinking that something was wrong, very wrong I had to know I didn't have any personal information on her but I'm sure it's in my database and Renee would certainly be familiar with that so I went back to the bedroom to awake her but after looking at her and how peaceful she was sleeping there were no signs of the chaotic event she had endured the previous day on her face at all I just couldn't bring myself to disturb her so I let her sleep. I so wanted to rejoin her thinking of how soft and beautiful her body is but business calls and my new partners are ready for action so I showered and begin preparing to conquer another day when I smelled the sweet aura of bacon and eggs in the air enticing my nostrils and seducing my taste buds, that completed the motivation I needed to put the sandman at rest for the day and I headed straight for the kitchen. Renee had just finished fixing our plates and breakfast never looked so good it was like looking at a vision of perfection, for a moment my mind was totally engross in the meal but when I looked up to thank Renee I saw her body completely naked for the first time and I must say it was flawless so hypnotic that I didn't even realize that I was staring,'you like' she said'I like'I said' do you want jelly on your toast'she ask'huh oh yeah right jelly' I managed to say somehow'is everything to your liking'she ask as she sat down to eat'huh oh everything to my liking yes'I uttered but this time with a little more awareness this meal will rank in my memory as the best I've ever experienced because every fiber of my being was being exploited my taste buds were enlighten my brains are working in full gear and my eyes are glued to Renee's remarkable shaped body there wasn't a part of me that wasn't happy at this moment. Once I had finished my meal Renee got up and cleared the dishes her nude body completely engulfed all of my brain cells if I didn't make love to her soon I was going to explode so I stood and walked up behind her as she was filling the dishwasher I put my arms around her waist and pulled her to me and as she turned toward me I kissed her passionately until she went limp in my arms, I picked her up and proceeded to the bedroom all the while telling her how I've longed for this moment and as I lowered her onto my bed I noticed she was crying'Renee what's wrong'I ask'nothing's wrong I've just longed for this moment too and now that it's here it's just a little overwhelming, Luke I'm in love with you I have been for a while now make me feel loved too'she said very sincerely I didn't say another word I removed my clothes and resumed kissing and touching her body leaving no part unattentive I made her womanhood my full focus and once we had both fulfilled our destiny she lay clinging to my body as if she never wanted this moment to end and I have to say that moment gave me a feeling of completion it was as if my whole world had taken on a new meaning'Luke I can't go back to him I don't love him anymore'Renee said'what do you want to do have you given it any thought'I ask'I've given it a lot of thought in fact I haven't been able to think of anything else'she told me'so what have you decided'I ask'I've decided to keep my job and quit him the only thing is I can't move in with my parents because they stay in another state I've met a few friends since moving here but they're his friends too my only other alternative is to get my own place but I'm so afraid of living alone do you have any suggestions'and she looked me straight in my eyes when she asked'Renee I love you but marriage would never work for me I'm a free spirit and I don't want to break your heart'I told her'let me worry about my heart I'm a big girl I know the risk and I'm not asking for marriage I've had enough of that for now I just want peace my mind mysoul my spirit and my body just want to experience peace, I want to wake up happy and go to sleep happy and baby you make me happy'she said'then let's do it'I said'if you need something from

'you can get your belongings from his house or you can start fresh I'll take you shopping so everything will be new'I told her but she didn't answer she just laid there clinging to me as if she was afraid to let go wow I thought what happened'you take all the time you need to decide but right now I've got to get to a meeting with our newest members Charlie and Ann Ferguson I have a special project for them and that reminds me the other one Patricia never made it to our dinner last night when you feel up to it would you find out why'I finished'I'm on it'said Renee as I pulled into the parking lot of the office building my phone ring 'yes'I answered''Mr Rich Charlie Ferguson''yes Charlie I'm entering the office building now I'll be there momentarily'I told him as I was getting off the elevator I saw Charlie and Ann pacing by my office door'a thousand pardons my secretary experience an emergency and needed my help but now that that issue is resolved let's get down to business''let's do that'Ann said so I unlocked my office and as we started to enter I heard what sounded like an explosion and then another one followed suit in fact it then seemed like an endless chain of them echo through my ear drums I remember unbearable pain as I was turning to see the cause of this noisy interruption, Charlie was sitting against the wall outside of my office door bleeding profusely his eyes were open but no sign of life registered, Ann was lying next to him crying like a baby I saw so much pain in her eyes as blood spilled from her abdomen the man that least the office across the hall from mine lay on his stomach motionless as did two other men who look like they had tried to run, my hip had a bullet hole in it that seemed to extend into my buttocks and as I was sinking to my knees I looked into the eyes of the man who was the cause of this calamity Renee's husband stood in the hallway holding what appeared to be an assault rifle I saw him turn and push the elevator's call button and then head for the stairs as he opened the door to the stairway my memory stopped. We were riding and decided to ask my uncle if we could use his restroom, after approaching his front door I knocked and knocked and said'I can see him in there but he won't answer'my brother John hollered'Clarence let us in we need to use your restroom'all the while tapping on the front window but still there was no answer so I stopped knocking trying to think of another place to relieve myself while John continued about then the front door opened and Clarence came out with a pistol in his hand and at that point I stepped backwards while Clarence turned toward my brother John with the gun aimed at the porch, he fired twice and then raised the gun's barrel toward John's abdomen and fired a third shot which seem to have sent my brother into a state of shock because he just stood there for what seemed like an eternity but of course was only seconds before grabbing his stomach and falling to the porch, my uncle's eyes never left his as the life exited my brother's body I had made it to the car about then and proceeded to back up to the neighbor's yard next door with the big wooden fence concealing my view, I tried to dial for help from a rotary operated cellphone not for emergency personnel but our mother and was unsuccessful so I decided to see what was happening on the porch where my brother's lifeless body lay, I pulled up in view of the crime scene and saw a hearse backing out of the yard with my brother John sitting upright in a casket in the rear, in the passenger seat I saw Clarence sitting with no life registering in his eyes either and right behind Clarence I saw Charlie and next to him was the guy who rented the office across from mine then I noticed two more figures which turned out to be the other men that had died in that hallway while trying to flee after the hearse cleared the driveway completely in the street it didn't puii forward as I was expecting instead it backed up next to the car I was in and that allowed me to see the driver, he was dressed in a black suit with a black hat his face was tar black and his eyes exhibited no sign of life they looked icy cold and once he had aligned his hearse along the side of my car he looked me straight in the eyes and said'I'll be back for you'and then he drove forward and as he did everyone in the hearse beginning with my uncle Clarence and ending with my brother John just stared at me as they passed, then they were gone just vanished, I kept looking but the hearse and all of it's occupants were nowhere to be seen and that's when I saw a little girl sitting on the curb across the street sobbing just then I awoke in a hospital with Renee at my bedside crying, I wanted to reach and grab her hand to comfort her but I was in no shape to move the pain even though I was very heavily medicated was awesome after Renee noticed my eyes were open I heard her say'oh my baby my sweet baby I'm so sorry please forgive me I will make this up to you, I will spend the rest of my life making this right in anyway you see fit just live my love please don't leave meenee's I don't want to live without you' Renee's words penetrated and nullified everything else even the pain didn't hurt as bad anymore she was amazing. But then her husband came to my mind and the pain began to increase again, flashbacks the memories came crushing through my brains like a Mack truck I began having an anxiety attack it became hard to breathe I remember hearing the machines that were monitoring my vitals going berserk I remember nurses entering my eyesight and working vigorously trying to stabilize me I remember thinking if I would actually get to enjoy this new found happiness that just entered my life or did that happiness cause my demise I remembered making mad passionate love to Renee and then I remembered all of the bloody bodies that caught my eyesight as I laid severely injured outside of my office door and then I remembered nothing everything went blank. Once unconsciousness had completely engulfed my mind I saw the guy in the black suit that had driven the hearse standing beside my bed looking me straight in the eyes this time he didn't say a word no word was needed his icy cold eyes said it all apparently my time was very near, I remembered all of the faces I had seen in the hearse and then it dawned on me that neither Ann or Patricia's face was among them which was strange to me because in some weird way it actually seemed like my nightmare was beginning to make some sort of sense. I awoke to Renee's caressing after seeing that I was awake she responded by kissing me on the cheek'hi baby welcome back'she said'how do you feel''I think I'll make it what time is it what day is it'I ask'it's Saturday night'she answered'Saturday I've been out for four days''I ask'yes it was touch and go for a while but you came out victorious'she said'what about Ann'I ask'she pulled through as well but Charlie lost the battle'she told me'and the others'I ask hoping that the nightmare of them in the hearse was just a nightmare'all of them gone'she answered'and your husband was he caught'I ask'yes he was and he's being held without bond I hope he burn'she added'he will'I said'one way or another did you find out why Patricia missed our dinner celebration''yes Patricia had her own tragedy that day after leaving the office she stopped to buy something special to wear and was robbed as she was leaving the robbers also took her car poor girl was bruised pretty badly'Renee added'how's she doing'I ask'well she's out of the hospital but mentally she's a wreck, I've tried calling and talking to her but she won't talk long and the little time she does is through teary eyes'Renee said and about that time a nurse entered my room and upon seeing that I was awake she said'welcome back Mr Rich'then proceeded to check all of the machines that were monitoring my condition'everything looks good how are you feeling'the nurse ask'oh I think I'll make it'I answered'your doctor will be here to see you in the morning and at that time we'll know more about your release date'the nurse said as she was exiting the room'great'I said and turned to look at Renee who was already looking at me, 'Luke I'm scared'don't be' I told her' now that I know how serious this situation is I'm going to handle it, believe me your husband will never hurt any of us again I promise you' and after assuring her I added' now I need to find out how Ann's doing and see what if anything we can do to make her pain a little easier'' I'm on it' Renee said then kissed me and left the room, I don't have to tell you that right now I'm pissed off ways of total destruction are flowing through my mind concerning Renee's husband I'm not going to take a chance that he will ever be a free man again, he has disrupted my life, my business and my money for this he was going to pay with his life. Well I guess it's about time to let all of you readers know the type of business I orchestrate the reason my partners have to be willing to travel at a moment's notice and unlimited flexible hours are a given is because I run Rich hit international which simply means assassinations, we are hired by the elite of the elite executing anyone from rival business partners to feuding family members, as head of the company I scan through the many requests and assign the right agents to handle very specific jobs I live very modest for cover but I'm actually as my last name indicates very, very rich, my business partners are investigated from the time they leave their mother's womb until they sign a contract with me which is why I knew something was wrong the night Patricia didn't show up for our dinner date. Charlie and Ann were precious because to hire a husband or wife usually causes conflict in the marriage at some point so to hire both of them is rare and a great combination for success because they can infiltrate scenarios that would otherwise be suspicious if attempted by a single assassin. My company is so camouflage that my partners and I rarely face opposition on or off an assignment so we were taken completely by surprise when that idiot of a husband went on his jealous killing spree and of course signed his death warrant in the process, the only reason he's still among the living is because I've been out of commission and none of my partners are going to hit him without my permission, but now that my head is clearing his life span has suddenly become very short. Renee only knows that each mission my partners complete net my company an enormous amount of money she has no idea of the activity that takes place during those missions, so as far as she will know someone killed her husband and left her a free woman I glanced at the time eleven fifth teen p.m. suddenly I felt extremely tired I'll grab a few hours of sleep and then prepare to squash the tiny bug that reek so much havoc and as I drifted

Yet I can't help but wonder what she would do if she knew the true purpose of my business, I knew with her as my wife I couldn't hide our livelihood from her permanently and I shouldn't have to because there shouldn't be any secrets between a man and his wife that would have to be a sure recipe for failure so I have to tell her soon because if she found out from another source that would destroy the real trust that a marriage should be built on and without that foundation the marriage would just be a charade. There are so many thoughts going through my mind right now that my brain is producing a migraine headache but I've got to deal with this predicament because I don't want to lose my girl, focus I had to keep telling myself you've got to stay focus, life was so much easier before I fell in love except for that nightmare I had it made, going through life giving account to no one but myself certainly had it's advantages but I have to admit I had more than my share of lonely times mix with them and now Renee has given my life a whole new meaning. I'm going to just straight up tell her point blank, she's either going to stand by me or I'm going to lose her damn I don't want to think about that but that's reality and I know it would be best for my heart, at least it could start the healing process instead of prolonging the matter and let it crush us both in the future, my thoughts were interrupted when Renee walked in looking like beauty itself I noticed she had freshen up, she smelled like a garden of freshly bloom flowers, yes I had to tell her there was no doubt about it but it definitely didn't have to be now, right now I think I'll just relax and enjoy this new world of joy that I've entered, I don't know what I did to deserve her and I've always been told not to look a gift horse in the mouth so I'm going to take her home and cherish her for a while'hi baby how you feeling'she ask'I'm good I think the doctor is going to release me today I hope anyway because I'd really like to start enjoying my life with you'I told her'and I you'she told me and then continued'I've been monitoring our business interest and business is good we're making a lot of money, Luke how exactly do we make our money I have no knowledge of our partners job description' I knew then that it was time to reveal the true nature of our success and said'I'll explain everything when we get home, I'd like to discuss it all in the privacy of our home''I'd like that'she said as she grabbed my hand and just held it, this is the life I thought I just hope she can deal with the truth. Finally the doctor entered the room and said'I'll bet you're ready to go home"'doc. I'm past ready'I answered 'well according to your vital signs and all of the test we did on you you're be leaving as soon as we can get your discharge papers ready which should only take a few minutes longer"'thank you doctor thanks for everything'I said'take care'he said as he walked out of the door and a feeling of relief came over me I can go home at last I thought. Renee had already got my clothes and was bringing them to me, then help me take off the hospital gown and slowly dressed me, once I was dressed we waited for the discharge papers which wasn't long in coming, after I was discharged we headed home with her driving of course, upon pulling into the driveway my sense of relief suddenly became an overwhelming burden of guilt, as we entered the house anxiety took my body and immobilized it, I just stood there'what's wrong baby'Renee ask'sit down we need to talk'I said and started from the beginning of how I laid the foundation for Rich hit international and built it into the fortress it is today leaving out no detail, I explained the role of each partner, how they were chosen and the reason they were given the mission assigned to them, I told her how much the company's gross and net worth were and with business in full bloom I needed more partners which explained the interviews and that the estimated profits from this quarter alone would solidify our standings of being among the elite of the elite, yes assassinations were in big demand especially among the very rich and once I had finished the full assessment of Rich hit international I had to sit down but the anxiety started to subside and I became mobile again. After sitting down I waited on a response

Hoping that even if she wasn't alright with it and knowing her I knew she wouldn't be, she would at least for our sake let it happen, but she just sat there expressionless, I mean completely blank and of course I began to fear the worst, suddenly she spoke very calm and collectively, 'you know I can't work for you any longer',' I'm not surprise 'I tried to say with dignity,'Luke why? Does money mean that much to you and if so what wouldn't you do for it? For some reason that question coming from her entered my ears and overloaded my brains, what wouldn't you do for money?wow then it dawned on me, I have people killed and that recurring nightmare entered my head about people close to me dying on a nightly basis, the pain I felt every time I saw my uncle murder my brother, the look in my brother's eyes as his life exited his body, the blank stare on my uncle's face as he stood there holding the murder weapon, the pain Ann exhibited as she grieve the death of her husband, the pain in the hospital room on Renee's face when she thought I was dying, the pain on her face now because she has to make a decision that's going to rip her heart apart and frankly I found it hard to look her directly in the eyes,'Luke I asked you a question, can't you even answer it, I love you baby but right now I need some space, I feel overwhelmed, I'm going to check into a hotel for tonight because I really need time to think'she said as tears were running down her face,'Renee please stay I'll leave, just call me when you're up to it'I pleaded with her, then as I started to leave she came and put her arms around my waist from behind and laid her head on my back for a long moment, then I turned around and was able to look her in the eyes again when I heard her say'don't leave my love, I don't agree with what you're doing but I don't want you to leave either, baby just hold me like you've never held me before'. So I held her it was like I could feel all of her emotions, love, confusion, indifference, disgust, loyalty, each one just as powerful as the other, that's when I picked her up and carried her to bed, slowly and thoroughly loving her mind, body and soul, taking away all her inhibitions and replacing them with feelings of security, letting her know that regardless of anything else she is my number one priority, my world, and that the love I had for her transcended life itself, an fulfilling unconditional love. Choosing between her and my company wasn't a contest at all, she made me happy and I hadn't been happy since childhood, she fell asleep in my arms and again no nightmares, when I awoke the next morning she was lying with her head on my chest as if she was listening to my heartbeat all the while studying my face as I slept,'good morning, you look gorgeous' I told her,'good morning' she said then continued,'Luke when I asked what you wouldn't do for money you never answered me so I'm going to ask a more direct question' I braced myself because I had a feeling this was going to hurt and hurt badly,'would you end us for money?','end us'I said a little confuse, then she continued'I can't marry you knowing how you make your fortune, but according to the financial records of the company's assets there's more than enough money to close and start fresh, there's so many other ways to keep your success in full gear, Luke would you do that for us?','you want me to sell my company?'I asked,'no just transfer your investment procedures'she answered,'then you'll marry me?',I asked'then I'll marry you'she answered,'I'll call my lawyers at once'I said,'I'm on it' she told me, and it didn't take long to see my solid fortress come tumbling down. once I got stronger we decided to go into the real estate business and Renee did a lot of non profit volunteering, we got married soon afterwards and that recurring nightmare stopped completely. Renee brought meaning back into my life, she is tireless never a dull moment, I surrounded myself with death so death surrounded itself with me until he even entered and controlled my dreams, but that part of my reality has ended, now I've jump on life's back and taking a ride I didn't know existed, consisting of love, joy, and total happiness, the kind a good woman radiates

Completion

-written by Rocky Earl Smith-a.k.a. darkbrain

I think of life, I think of death, I think of motives, I think of solutions, I think of journeys, I think of adventures, but most of all I think of completion, that's my absolute focus, completion in life doesn't mean that it's over, it just mean that if for some reason the journey does end, I'm alright with that.

Assorted Inputs

written by\Rocky Earl Smith

Dispute This

Déjà vu-sounds familiar, when we feel we've experienced what seems to be an exact event before, it happens and it's too real to dismiss, there are different scientific theories explaining why it happens. Reincarnation has long been one of those seemingly logical answers, I'm not disputing it but going through life dying, being born again and experiencing the same events each lifetime seems redundant, but that's just my opinion. Lately I've been doing extensive research on the origin of the universe and the idea scientist agree the most on is the big bang theory, although no one can explain how zero volume became total existence, but that's still the most popular diagnosis. A creator-seems to be the most logical yet illogical reasoning as to how the event took place, and again I'm not disputing that belief either but it still doesn't explain repeated exact experiences. Parrellel Universes-what if there is a multiverse, where more than one universe exist, then that would give way to the extensive arguments of multiple realms or dimensions, one theory is that matter can only arrange itself into so many forms before it has to start repeating the process, what if matter produce another one of each of us in other dimensions and what if that version of us had all of the same characteristics, in essence they are us, wouldn't it stand to reason that similar experiences and memories are inevitable. Then at some point these universes intertwine with one another and the us in that realm experience the same event as the us in this dimension and say simultaneously déjà vu, seriously what if.

The Multidimensional Elevators

written by Rocky Earl Smith- a. k. a.-Darkbrain

'It's perfect' said Jack the engineer who designed the two hundred story building, 'my critics laughed at me saying building this tower would be impossible, but here it stands, solid and unyielding from the ground all the way to the rooftop and now to make known that the world's tallest building is open for business, the penthouse suites will bring in a fortune by themselves, imagine room service it will be like being waited on by angels and eating with the gods themselves, get the press here at once' Jack concluded,' not so fast' replied Prince the owner of the new tower,' I want to take one more tour just for my own satisfaction,' so the two of them entered the freshly built elevator,' we're going directly to the roof and descend from there,' the prince said and with that he placed a key into a special slot into the elevator's control panel which allowed them to bypass the two hundred floors and proceed directly to the roof, and once reaching the designated level the elevator was stopped and the two men stepped off and began their final tour of approval, examining every inch of the roof making sure all mechanisms were working properly and then they started their descent. Going from one floor unto the other covering every room with detailed precision until finally they were back in the lobby exhausted,' Now' the prince began to say,' Let's start the marketing process,' and before long the press from every major advertising agency was there, television networks, radio broadcasters, newspapers and magazines, not to mention social media all sent representatives to cover a part of history in the making, a building of this magnitude was the top news of the day, everyone anxious to see who would be the first guests in the hotel among the stars, yes it was literary among the stars, it stretched so far into the night sky it was like you could step out of a penthouse suite and onto a star and sure enough once word got out that it was open for business, reservations began flowing in from all over the world. Dignitaries, the elite of the elite, everyone wanted a penthouse suite, others were content just to experience the freshness of the rooms in which all of the latest technology known to man dwelt and it wasn't long before the hotel was at full capacity with reservations pretty much the same. With all the technology on hand the hotel had very little need for human employees, so the service was self induced even the room service needed no outside contributions, the guest controlled everything, whatever they desired in their world while they occupied the room was pretty much granted, it was perfect

The owner had spared no expense, the engineer had designed it precisely and the builders were all top notch workers who took great pride in their professionalism all of them knowing that this project could lead to a lot of big opportunities. The hotel was such an exciting experience that it became very difficult to vacant the ones occupying the suites so others who had reservations could start their stay, no one wanted to leave and of course this eventually became a big problem. How do you tell the elite of the elite that their money is no good, that others with just as much or more are expecting the rooms that they're occupying, they plainly disregard anyone needs outside of their own, in fact once word spread about the difficulty of changing occupants because of the rewarding stay incoming reservations were requested as indefinite ones and that tended to reduce the problems of rollover stays. Yes the owner had invested well and it paid off immensely, his profits skyrocketed at a very rapid rate and they easily made him the richest man on the planet by far and of course he became very famous, things couldn't have been better for the prince he was on top of the world. There were so many floors in his hotel that it took multiple elevators to service them, fifty of them as a matter of fact and they each ran without ceased so maintenance was of the uppermost importance and again the prince spared no expense, he was a shrewd businessman whose number one rule was it takes money to make money so he had no problem investing in the best, even the elevators were futuristic, the guess had only to speak their destination and the elevators got them there with complete ease and if they wanted entertainment during their short trip they had only tell the elevator what they desired whether it was music or video in fact any particular sound that would soothe their mind or motivate their psychic they were granted. The elevators were so loaded with the best of technology that the guess were made very relaxed and comfortable, it was like they had a mind of their own, the conversations that took place between them and the guess was very explicit it was like talking to the desired person, a friend, family member, a spouse, siblings, children, even mentors, sometimes when the passenger arrive at their appointed floor they find it difficult to exit the elevator because of the joyous experience that they just encountered, all fifty elevators were exquisive

Exquisite but one of them was without a doubt the cream of the crop, number twenty three, this elevator used it's technology to create magical moments, for example as one of the guest in the hotel was riding after checking in the conversation veered toward a historic moment that he couldn't get out of his memory because of the traumatic event that had taken place and then as the elevator approached the floor of the suite the guest had reserved tears began falling in waves down his face so much so that elevator number twenty three began to work it's magic and the man suddenly felt very strange and then a feeling of calm and similarity came over him and the whole scenario changed and as the view became clearer the man was suddenly terrified with fear and disbelief, the past event he had discussed with the elevator had somehow become a present reality everything as he remembered it down to the last detail, it was like he had stepped back in time revisiting a very traumatic moment, the man closed his eyes, rubbing them, open them and blinked a few times thinking he had somehow fell asleep on the ride up, but not so he was awake and helpless to change what was unfolding before him, the same people, same age, the same features and conversation just as he remembered them, and the emotions, it was like hitting a replay button to a nightmare, but then he realized that now he actually had a second chance, he didn't understand how such a transformation was even possible, but he would try and figure that out at a later time as for right now he focus his mind on correcting the wrong that would haunt him from this day forward because he knew in his being that whatever caused his present dimension to overlap his past at the precise time of that life altering moment was without a doubt only a temporary ordeal, so the man without further hesitation and not to mention no viable options greeted the characters, the man Henry Ross, his mother Beatrice, his sister Camille, and his dad Henry Sr., the place the family home, the time the year 1992, the scene another fierce argument between his parents over finances, the man now age 16 was trying to finish his homework with visions in his head of graduating soon and moving far away from all of this chaos, his sister Camille a year older 17 had had enough and was in the midst of packing only essentials in her determination to vacate the premises at once, his parents fight was so heated that neither of them noticed as their daughter headed toward the door with suitcase in hand until she opened the door to leave and a cold blast of wintered chilled air lowered their body temperatures, 'Camille get back in here at once,' her daddy screamed,' Camille, honey where are you going,' her mother whimpered,

'Shut up I got this' Henry Sr. Told his wife as he slapped her hard across the face, Camille was furious,' Leave my mother alone,' she shouted as she charged toward her dad, but without much effort Henry Sr. Shrugged her sending her tumbling to the floor,' Now you listen to me,' her daddy growled,' I want that suitcase unpacked and you are to stay in your room until I say otherwise do you understand me,'' No' Camille screamed,' I'm leaving and you can't stop me, I've had enough, this constant bickering is driving me nuts, I can't handle it anymore,' but before Camille could finish her statement her dad grabbed her and began dragging her by the hair across the floor toward her room as she struggled to free herself crying and scratching at his hand,' Leave her alone,' Beatrice shouted,' take your hands off of my daughter,' this infuriated Henry Sr. To no limit so he threw Camille into her bedroom slamming the door and then returned and resumed assaulting his wife but this time he didn't stop at slapping her he began to beat her and the look in his eyes was unrecognizable, she soon started to succumb to the onslaught and although Henry Jr. Remembered what had happened the first time around he found himself repeating history but this time knowing in his heart that no other choice was available as he heard his sister's life curling scream as she jumped on her father's back scratching and biting and hitting trying to stop him from beating her mother because she knew her mother couldn't take much more of this abuse, but her father hit her so hard that he knocked her across the room and her head hit the corner of the coffee table sending her into unconsciousness and then he turned his attention back to his unconscious wife, Henry Sr. Was like a man possess, the sight of the two women dearest to him lying helpless on the floor didn't faze him in the least he was without remorse. But the onslaught stopped that is until he heard his wife groan in agony and then he kneeled beside her and began beating her again, and that's when Henry Jr. Ran over to his father grabbed him and the two began tussling with both of them delivering some awesome punches hurting each other quite a bit, but soon Henry Jr realized that he was no match for his father and his mind flashed back to the first time this scene took place, the argument, the beatings placed on his mother and sister, the assault on him, and then he thought of the reason he had wished for this moment again because he felt that there had to have been something he could have done to make things turn out different because he loved his father so much, but now that he found himself at the moment of truth, the moment that would forever change the outcome of his life, he knew that what happened the first time would happen over and over regardless of how many times the overlap dimensions would merge, fate had sealed this part of his history, he would again kill his father and with that thought the elevator stopped on the floor to the room Henry Ross had reserved, with elevator number twenty three announcing it's arrival and as he exited in search of his room number his mind had a renewed view of that life shattering event that forever change the course of his destiny, though the thought of what happen that day still saddened him it no longer haunted him.

Meanwhile as another guest talked with elevator twenty three she was captivated by it's charm and felt the need to open up and spill some emotions, she was an high priced first class escort and though she hated her livelihood it allowed her to enjoy the finer things in life, she was nobody's fool but because of her job description she was a very lonely woman and of course trusted no one. But there was something about the elevator's conversation that took her emotionally to a time in her past when life was an happy existence, a time when she was surrounded by family and friends, it wasn't as glamorous but there was joy in her heart, these feelings filled every inch of space in elevator number twenty three and the elevator began to work it's magic, the characters Keisha Perkins, the woman, her mother Kathy and sister Katrina, the place the town home the three shared together, the year 2005, Keisha 15 at the time, her sister 12 going on 18 in her head she was very mature for her age and their mother were as content as a family could be and there wasn't a huge gap between the ages of mother and sisters because Keisha was born when her mother was 14 years old also very mature for her age even though she was gullible to smooth talking boys she decided to keep her babies regardless of the major obstacles that tried to prevent that from happening and now at age 29 Kathy even without a major education made a decent life for her girls, there were so many material things she couldn't give them but the love that radiated from every fiber of her being couldn't have been deeper. Keisha was transformed on every level as her present dimension overlap with her past, in fact it felt so natural to her that she totally embraced the reality, she never wanted it to end, it was like she had died and went to heaven, talking to her mom again spending time with her sister this time not in a reminiscing sense but in reality. The elevator allowed her to enjoy that sense of fulfillment for an extended period of time before delivering her to the floor she had requested at which point the dimensions separated and the present again became the path she had chosen for herself in order to compensate for the lack of love she now experienced in her life, the woman stepped off of the elevator and never looked back, she would never forget what happened during that short trip but she knew in her heart that it was best that she leave it there and focus on what she had to do to maintain. Time passed without elevator number twenty three working it's magic, because of multiple riders people chose not to have deep conversations while others were present and for the most part that was always the case but at some point technology at it's best would dutifully be tested and due to the exceptional list of riders with guilt stricken past all 50 of the elevators experienced mind altering talks with a host of guests, but elevator number twenty three was the only one of them that could combine the latest technology with multi dimensional magic. On one occasion the prince himself was enroute and having a very intelligent conversation and for some reason he began talking about how it had all began, his personal journey from humble beginnings to becoming by far the richest man on the planet, his success was so unique that the elevator itself was in awe of his accomplishments and the obstacles he had to overcome to get where he is. But even as awesome as the prince journey had been there was still a moment in his past that he dreaded and wished he had it to do over again and as if on cue elevator number twenty three began working it's magic, the characters, the prince alone with his business partner Frank, and Frank's wife Angela, the place the prince and Frank's real estate office, the year 1995, the scenario celebrating the start of the new year after a very victorious business quarter which made the two of them very rich. The celebration went from their office to include as much of the city as they could cover and then to the prince's estate where even more drinking and celebrating took place until the three of them had reached their limit at which point Frank and Angela decided to head home, the prince knowing what had happened to them previously invited them to spend the night

And go home the next morning once they had sobered up, but Frank's mind having been totally confiscated by alcoholic spirits insisted that he was capable of driving them home and at that point the prince recommended calling a taxi telling Frank that he was too drunk to drive, but Frank became even more persistent and in a very angry tone told the prince to mind his own business, that would have been the end of the argument if the prince hadn't known what was about to take place but that knowledge prompted his following actions as he reached for Frank's keys in an attempt to take them away from him which led to the wrestling match between the two in which the smaller man not to mention him being sloppy drunk himself was no match for the larger one even though he was fighting to save his friend's life, and soon Frank and his wife Angela was seated in his vehicle about to fulfill the path fate had ordained for them. The prince remembered hearing the roar of Frank's engine as it disrupted the calmness of the quiet night which he later called the sound of death and then as the sound got farther and farther away it became just a faint echo and it saddened the prince when the realization dawned on him that even though he had gotten another chance to stop the tragic event that had haunted him for the past thirty years he had failed, he now realized that fate was a powerful foe, the prince's journey of success had been a rigid but unequaled one, he hadn't tasted defeat for a long time but now he understood that once fate had sealed an event no one or nothing could change it and his last thoughts as the elevator stopped at his destination was of the lives that were lost that night because of drunk driving and even though his success still exceeded all expectations he couldn't help but wish Frank was around to enjoy it with him and needless to say the prince never consumed another drop of alcohol after that fateful night. Elevator number twenty three knew that the overlapping of dimensions giving people another chance to correct a part of their past that disturbed them would never change the outcome of the event because simply put the past can't be changed, but the elevator did find it necessary in some cases to let certain people go back for their own good, it was the only way some of them would stop living in the past and began to fully embrace their future. The elevator knew that so far the humans it had encountered from guest of the hotel to employees and even the owner himself all had at least one scenario in their past that they felt they could correct if given a second chance, no one was immune and so the elevator would grant them that opportunity and even though nothing changed most were grateful because they at least knew that it was nothing they could have done to alter the outcome of that dreadful event. So when this war veteran unloaded an experience unfamiliar to the elevator's previous recollections the elevator of course worked it's magic, the characters, the war veteran Sergeant Charlie Pointer, his commanding officer, Captain John Seevers and the rest of his platoon, the place Iraq, the year 1997, the war has been brutal as a whole but on this particular day the enemy soldiers were relentless, Sergeant Pointer had his orders to attack the rear of the enemy's line but the soldiers anticipated the move and were waiting, Sergeant Pointer and his men though fully alert were overcome but when Captain Seevers and his regiment attacked the frontline with everything they had being launched at the enemy this gave Sergeant Pointer and his remaining men a chance to regroup and all together release all of the fire power in their arsenal, but the enemy was everywhere it was as if fate had brought them all here to die and the Sergeant watched in horror as the Captain's head landed on the ground before his body realized it was missing and then his body followed suit and covered his head as it hit the ground, there were troops trying to maintain the fight, there were other troops lying injured on the ground some with missing body parts, some insides was fully exposed to the elements, some death had already claimed but some was amazingly clinging to life. The Sergeant was now in command due to the death of Captain Seevers so when he saw that his remaining troops didn't have a chance of winning this battle he gave the order to retreat trying to save as many of his fallen comrades as possible, but the problem was in trying to save the injured the retreating soldiers were being slaughtered until Sergeant Pointer was all that remained and was taken as a P.O.W., again a prisoner of war was the thought pounding in his head as he realized his predicament, this scenario was going to turn out exactly as it had before with him becoming a war hero but always asking why, why did all the men in his division die except him, the guilt would haunt him for the rest of his life and without thinking Sergeant Pointer seeing one of the enemy soldiers relieving himself made a dash for his weapon and upon retrieving it he opened fire killing as many of their soldiers as possible before a hail of returned enemy fire gave him the ending he sought, and as he lay dying the pain took second place to the satisfaction he felt, his last thoughts were that this is how it's suppose to end with me dying in the same battle with all of my friends and fellow comrades and then he was gone, so when elevator number twenty three arrived on the war hero's designated floor no one exit because no one had entered, his place in history had changed because he was granted a second chance, so when the overlap dimensions did resume their natural course Sergeant Charlie Pointer remained in the former and elevator number twenty three stored all in his memory tanks, in fact this last encounter in which fate was defeated weighed in on the elevator's magic, the multi dimensional overlap trips now took on a dimension in itself, nothing was sacred. The elevator was very hesitate from that day forward as to who it granted second chances, knowing the replications of such acts could be dire, totally changing history is not just an individual adjustment but it changes the history of everyone connected to that account, and it doesn't take a genius to figure out that allowing people a chance to change their fate will at some point lead to disaster, so the elevator decided that for the sake of stability it would stop the practice of displaying it's magic and to this day it has never granted a second chance to anyone. Anyone that would read about that particular battle that took place during the Iraq war would read that there were no survivors. The End

My Dreams

written by Rocky Earl Smith

In my dreams I see a world of total beauty, there's beauty in the oceans, the mountains, the desserts, the entire landscape. In my dreams I feel fair weather, winter, spring, summer and fall, in my dreams all fowl, all animals, all sea dwelling creatures, live, play and survive in perfect harmony. In my dreams humankind, though still having so many problems and unresolved issues, find a way to stamp out war and crime and poverty, imagine my disappointment when I awoke in the same nightmare that I fell asleep in, then I pondered the question I've pondered so many times before, can dreams come true ?will my dreams ever come true?Imagine world peace, Imagine world love, they're in my dreams

The World Within the World

written by Rocky Earl Smith-a.k.a. darkbrain

'This is a very competitive life'shouted G as it fought S for possession of Ed's heart cells'it's getting to the point that every move is challenged, no longer is the body's immune system our only enemy now there's an abundance of enemies fighting for every organ in everybody regardless of it's genetic makeup. I remember when organs were plentiful, there were enough for all of us, but now with so many more of us in existence living unoccupied cells are hard to find'G stated as it's struggle became harder'I can't do this anymore I've gotten too old and too weak to compete against these superpowered germs, I'm just going to go into my final stage and consume whatever is available after all else feast'G completed as S stripped the cells from Ed's heart from it's grip. G retreated into the atmospherics vacancies feeling humiliated and worthless, not to mention extremely hungry. B witnessed the entire struggle and approached G with a proposition 'that was a good fight the same thing not only happened to me but keep happening much too frequently''yea beat it I've got my own problems if I don't get some nutrition in me soon it won't matter' G said 'then listen I've got the answer, there are a lot of us that's becoming obsolete, my suggestion is we band together for the sake of our survival, it's our best no I'll go even father and say it's our only chance because these new super germs are killing all of us indirectly but if we joined forces that would level the battlefield and enhance our meal production'B stated'hmm' G said'that just may work besides I don't really see much of an alternate but if we're going to act we have to do it soon otherwise I won't be much help I'm deteriorating as we speak'G told him'fine I've already devised a plan so let's round up the rest of our gang members and attack those super germs'said B. As B was introducing G to the rest of it's clan G sensed a lack of motivation among the aging germs it was no secret that none of them wanted to tangle with the young super germs but they knew their chance of survival depended on it so reluctantly it was agreed that all would band together. B led the group as they searched for the easiest prey possible but was soon to learn there was no such thing, the super germs had spread their powerful bacteria on a seemingly infinite scale and everyone in the aging group of germs came to the realization that their mission of survival looked very grim so grim that fear gripped their whole being, but regardless of the odds they were warriors, to fight gave them a chance even if it was slim to none so fight they would and at B's command they acted as one and swarmed the human cells with all they could muster attempting to drive the super germs that had taken residence in them out so the battle began, with B at the helm the aging germs fought and fought and fought, the super germs had underestimated the former reigning army but adjusted well, their youth definitely gave them the advantage, but the one thing none of them had anticipated was that their battle proved fatal to the cells that each wanted to possess and of course if enough of the cells die the organs start to malfunction which eventually leads to the death of the subject, this became a regular occurrence as the war raged on and soon the number of casualties began reaching a very alarming capacity which led to special interest groups focusing solely on the matter. The leaders of the germ world knew that humans dying at this rate was not sustainable so with the up most of reservations they agreed to hold a meeting and discuss this tragic dilemma. B and G being the leaders of the aging class of germs met with S the leader of the super germs and of course the tension in the meeting place was undeniable at the highest level possible. G started the discussion'this is a problem that's impossible to ignore, by combating one another for living cells we're destroying the very nutrients we all need to survive, if we continue at this pace human cells will become extinct and we all know that if that happens we're soon become extinct as well having nothing to feed on so for the sake of our continued existence I suggest we form a union and find a way in which we can all survive'the leader of the super germs remained silent for a moment as if in deep concentration and this made B respond'I would advise you to accept the deal we're offering even though your species is more powerful than ours overall we as a combined adversary are leveling the field to the point that if we can't survive no one will'still S remained silent for a moment more before answering the pack of germs that in his view are just misfits'first of all for you to even think we would consider forming a union with a bunch of has beens like you is comical but you are right the battle at hand is not sustainable therefore we will change our tactic, from this point forward we will cast a direct attack against your species wiping you out of existence leaving us the superior germ fare supreme'then as soon as it had completed it's statement the S super germs were attacking the aging B nd G germs without mercy, you see the slaughter had been planned before the meeting right down to the last detail, the age germs were no fools though they knew something like this was possible even likely so they had concocted a form of defense in anticipation, but the S germs were relentless destroying the army of aging germs with the skills of the super beings they were, even with the plan of defense the aging germs were fighting a losing battle but they fought anyway mainly because they had no choice in the matter, turning and fleeing wasn't an option the speed of the super germs out matched them as well although a few of them tried to no avail. The leaders of the B and G species of germs were both slaughtered at the point of attack and after a valiant attempt at surviving the remaining members of the aging armies followed suit, then as the super germs looked about admiring their handy work their leader spoke'fools, they were all fools to think that we as the superior germ would share anything with their declining species and now that we have annihilated them let's feast'and with that they proceeded to pounce on every living cell possible. But as they were enjoying the unchallenged feast there soon became another problem, a new germ was suddenly invading the overflow of living cells, they were totally different from the enemies the S germs had just faced in the fact that they were younger and much stronger, they soon became known as the Z germs and even though the S germs felt they were the most powerful species of germs in existence they somehow had a very uneasy feeling about these newly formed adversaries, and that feeling soon became justified because these newly formed species of germs were like no others the S clan had ever encountered. These Z germs excelled in every aspect, taking over the S clan territory and robbing them of their now self proclaiming title of super germs because these Z germs were complete they not only feast on living cells but dead cells as well and this combination somehow made them immune to any resistance, this included the S now former super germs, of course they wouldn't give up their crown without a serious fight so they fought with a vengeance but to no avail, the Z species of germs had no problem annihilating their entire population in record time, the leader of the S clan was the last to succumb to the rigorous onslaught and it's last thoughts were [damn] and the S germ species became a part of history. The Z species caused world chaos they appeared invincible, the leader of the species decided that it's army would be even powerful if they were split into different forms, so it appointed a deadly virus team whose total responsibility would be to attack the immune system of all living cells, the next team was a deadly disease squad whose responsibility would be to destroy any powerful medications created to combat the viruses and the remaining Z germ army was assigned the responsibility of destroying any and all germs new or already in existence making sure that their species would remain without question supreme on every level and the plan worked to perfection as each team excelled at their assignments, humans, animals, fowls, reptiles, no form of life was exempt, even after the living cells died the Z germs would feast still, it was unheard of, these were monstrous almost robotic entities it was as if their creator had taken very exquisite designs in it's thoughts at their creation. Scientist were baffled nothing seemed to even faze let alone slow down the pace of destruction that these now given name by all that feared them [death spell]the world called for unity, leaders sought other leaders assistance, allies made pacts with sworn enemies vowing to put all differences aside until they could be assured that life on earth would remain intact, everyone sought solutions, cures had to be found and found quickly if mankind would survive, it was like the world became one, as with one thought, one focus, one purpose, no expense was spared in man's quest to stop the destroyer known as death's spell. But as time passed and the population of earth dwindle at every level widespread panic became the norm, undertakers couldn't keep up with demand, funeral homes were over logged, new grounds were constantly prep for graveyards in fact now every section of every city had multiple graveyards either under construction or already sold out. The leader of the Z clan was so delighted in it's many victories that it failed to notice a newly form species of germs it would soon become to know as the X germs, the X species unlike the Z clan didn't arrive in a grandstand instead they were a laid back easy going clan of micro bytes, they were fully aware of the chaotic havoc the Z germs posed but didn't appear to take it to heart, in fact even though their leader knew the Z clan history and saw the extent of their powers seemed unfazed and frankly unimpressed because it fitted in perfectly with the X clan agenda.

Puzzled well let me put things in perspective you see the X germs were not interested in feasting on living or dead cells, they're not even remotely interested in doing battle with the Z clan or any other species of germs, no none of those things matter to these newly formed micro bytes, these germs are truly different from their counterparts in a way totally unheard of before their creation these germs are cannibals, yes you read it right these newly formed X species of germs feast exclusively on other germs which will prove to be a very defying chain of events. First of all the fact that the X clan is so laid back cause the Z clan not to take them very seriously, but by the Z clan being the most feared army roaming the biosphere they of course kept tabs on all potential enemies and the X clan was no exception, but the X germs played their role well, their lack of activity and seemingly lack of interest prompted the Z clan leader to somewhat begin to underestimate them and that was the X germ leader's plan, it had anticipated an break and it didn't come a moment too soon because as leader of this cannibalistic army of beings it knew that the time to feast was upon them, they had managed to keep their eating habits very secretive and it had been very slim picking, lately the leader had been subject to mumbling from many unhappy members so much so that it has become impossible to ignore so a plan was devised and ready to be implemented, a plan that was about to change the whole path of reality for the entire germ world. The leader of the Z clan was calculus, he estimated complete rule of the entire globe would take place in a matter of days as it's three stage assault team escalate their advance, the leader of the X clan saw this as an opportunity to implement it's own plans because it knew that in order for the Z germ leader to escalate their advance they would have to expand their territory and to do that would mean the three deadly assault teams would face greater separation which left the more vulnerable one to it's X army attack which would also let them feast and regain their strength. They would start with team three the protectors whose team included the leader himself, so the leader of the X clan made sure it's full army knew their assignments they was about to feast on the most powerful species of germs in the known biosphere and that left no room for mistakes, but as each of them thought of the soon to be meal they couldn't help drooling in anticipation, when their leader saw what was happening he cautioned them not to think with their bellies but with their minds, it would be their only chance for success then after they were level headed again the plan was implemented. Converging as a force of one they approached team three of the Z germ clan with awesome precision and the war was on, the leader of the Z clan was no fool, after noticing their approach it directed it's followers to prepare for battle and what a battle it was, the Z clan was trained in every aspect of warfare, their knew all of the deadly points their opponents possess and wasted no time displaying their skills, their tactic proved worthy of notice by the X clan species of germs, but while the Z clan knew all of the killing bite points that had won them so many victories in the past this battle was different, the army they fought now was like none they had ever faced before, because this species of germs didn't try to bite certain areas to kill their prey, every bite no matter where it landed was lethal because they were cannibals, this gave the X clan the advantage, so it really didn't matter that they were greatly out matched in the skill of battle because they literally took a bite out of their enemy with every strike so needless to say that soon there were no enemies left to fight, excuse me eat and that included the Z clan's leading commander, team three of the fierce assault quad was now just a tongue licking memory to the now victorious species of X germs and with the memory of the feast still fresh on their taste buds the leader directed it's army to rest so they would be ready for their next battle or feast against team two which now delighted all of the X germs thoughts.

The annihilation of Z team three didn't go unnoticed by it's other two teams which led to them combining forces and choosing a new commander, the new commander vowed revenge for it's fallen, uh eaten comrades, the mood among them was vicious, the Z clan had ruled the micro world for some time now and the thought of being dethrone was unrealistic, the X germs would soon know who the true victors are and their punishment would be the hardest torture ever dealt to any foe, a punishment that will send a message to the entire micro world stating that the Z clan is in total control and always will be and that anyone that crosses them would suffer the same fate of utter defeat and annihilation. This message had to be administered without delay so the combined forces of the Z clan set out to find and stamp out the X germ species and needless to say the X germs were not hard to find in fact they had begun their search of the remaining members of the Z clan, so each army approached the other both focus on the total destruction, yet their method, their reasoning was as different as night and day, the Z clan wanted the sweet taste of revenge while the X germs just wanted the sweet taste, they couldn't stop their mouths from slobbering and their lips from smacking as the memory of their last battle flashed through their minds, their taste buds still savored the flavor of the Z clan's fallen comrades so much so that they soon found it hard to concentrate on the task at hand, but their leader notice the problem at once and immediately reminded them of the danger of not being totally focus and then led the charge not giving their minds a chance to idle again and the Z clan followed suit, both sides charged with the determination of the warriors they were. As they got closer the X army noticed something different about these remaining members of the Z species which made them look like a completely new enemy, nothing like their previous foes, you see these germs duties plagued living cells with viruses and diseases so it was only a matter of time before they mutated, and their mutated state completely change their appearance, their size, their weight and this change took an already super class of germs and made them even more powerful so as they neared the X clan of germs they towered over them and even though they still saw the Z germs as tasty meals suddenly their own well being became a concern, looking at these huge monstrous giants hovering over them their thoughts became confused, the memory of their last scrumptious encounter suddenly dwindled and more than a few of them began thinking that they had bit off more than they could chew. The X germ leader though a certain amount of confusion and doubt had consumed his mind as well it knew that there was no point dwelling on that fact, there was no time, in seconds the clash between the two armies would take place and it knew that if confusion and doubt had crossed it's mind then it stood to reason that it had cross some if not all of it's troops minds as well, it would have loved to have been able to turn to it's troops and motivate their confidence but there just wasn't enough time in fact before it even completed it's thoughts the battle was on. The Z now mutated super germs were an seemingly unstoppable force, they literary ripped the X germs apart, the X clan fought back as best as they could but were no match for this new brand of species because now in their mutated state the Z clan not only feasted on living cells but living germs as well, yes their mutation had made them cannibals and it didn't take long for this news to reach the entire biosphere spreading a new form of fear, a fear that prompted the rest of the micro world to put their differences aside and join forces in eliminating these two cannibalistic clan of germs while they were still in battle with each other, they reasoned that it would be their only chance of survival. It didn't take long to rally the armies for the cause of annihilating the cannibals, they were fed up with the X germs feasting on them and just as fed up with the Z clan not allowing them to feast, so this would be the perfect time for their assault now that they were battling each other. The war soon encamped the whole biosphere and what a battle it became, the X germs somewhat welcomed the intrusion because they were getting their butts whipped, the Z clan was taken by surprise because they didn't figure any of the microbytes had the courage to stand up against them, but despite everything the battle took on a whole new twist, living cells in all forms were taking advantage and blossoming, it was like all sicknesses, viruses, and diseases completely vanished from the earth's atmosphere, the inner biosphere and the underworld for the first time since man rebel had a clean bill of health flourishing throughout the entire population of the earth's inhabitants, and of course this baffled all concern but it was as welcomed as the precious gift that it was. Little did life on earth know it but this good fortune would continue for as long as the entire micro world was engaged in that horrific war, the germs fought relentless, the clash was furious with all involved knowing that defeat was not an option, this fight was for all the marbles with the victors resuming their rightful place in the biosphere and the losers ceasing to exist. The X germs was a formidable foe but was the first to go, their last thoughts as they vanquished were of how hungry they were, but the battle raged on between the new mutants and the rest of the germ world, where they fought and fought and fought with the Z clan having the advantage because they could keep their strength up by literary eating as many of the rest of the germs as they saw fit while the rest of the microbytes due to the length and viciousness of the war were beginning to get hungry and faint, once the leader of the Z clan saw that the battle had turned in his favor it ordered it's troops to a full scale attack of the weaker germs so this madness could end and it's army did as they were instructed with ultimate precision, the massacre took place swiftly and mercilessly, the Z clan killed and feasted like the monsters they had become, the pleasure they were experiencing at this moment superceded any they had ever felt, they stood victorious, they felt full, they were enjoying it so immensely that none of them notice that this war of wars, this ultimate and total defeat of the micro world had offset the laws of nature, their need to totally dominate and have absolute rule over the bio world were in violation of the laws that govern the world within the world and nature was furious'how dare you'said the voice heard throughout the biosphere, the Z clan went from wild celebration to immobile fear, helpless to do anything but listen and needless to say the rest of the germ world welcomed the intervention, then the voice was heard again'Z clan hear me, I have found you in violation and my patience has expired, you have disrupted all of the rules I have put in place to govern your tiny world and I find it unforgivable, therefore will my judgment be swift and without mercy, as of this moment the biosphere will return to it's former existence and that will happen without your presence'and with that the voice ceased and when the voice stopped the rest of the microbytes were astonished as they looked around and saw not one Z germ in the whole bio world, it was as if the voice took them with it, but then after the formal shock had subsided a great cheer echoed throughout the world within the world, this was truly a miraculous event for the germ world but not so much for living cells as the microbytes began to feast like nature intended them to do. Never again did one species of germs seek total domination, the story of the fate of the super powered Z clan was passed down from generation to generation warning all not to defy nature's laws, the consequences were too dire

King Satan

written by-Rocky Earl Smith\ a.k.a. Darkbrain

From the time I was created, I sought to take the throne
With my ego fully elated, I declared the system was wrong
I refuse to serve anyone, I think all should serve me
You'll see when I'm done, I'm the greatest there'll ever be
I rule an army of demons, I took them from God himself
With still some confuse sons, among the ones he has left
Soon I'll be in total control, all will bow at my command
Then each and every soul, will praise my name King Satan

Everything is so new to me yet I'm in sink with it all, everytime I'm
summoned by the most high I shine, at his command power surge my
entire being, his will is why I was created and is so satisfying that I
devote my whole focus to it, he's even assigned an multitude of angels
to assist me in his quest, I soak up the attention and yearn for more,
but I must resist my will of seeking more, I was created for the sole
purpose of doing the most high bidding and that role I do well. On
one occasion while communicating with the angels at my command I
was summoned to his presence, but for some reason I didn't respond
immediately as I'd always done, I was so into the conversation with
the angels that unconsciously I ignored the message and then I
noticed that I was talking to no one, the other angels had gathered
before the most high and was in position when I arrived, once there
it seemed like the rejoicing was based on my presence, my role was
very important, so I performed well. That was when my thoughts

took over my reality, when my ego set me up for the life of the outcast, it somehow changed my whole view as to who should really be in charge because I started thinking that everything centered around me and if that was the case then I should assume my rightful place, sure the most high created me but I was put here to rule. It took eons but some of the angels began to see things from my point of view and now with these new found followers I was actually beginning to feel empowered, but I knew that even as vast as this kingdom was there was only room for one king, so somehow I had to dethrone the creator himself. The question was how, the most high was just that the most high, how could I possible defeat the creator of all including myself, I pondered that question for eons more meanwhile growing unhappier with each summons, it got harder and harder to perform my duties with the attitude I now possessed and I knew that if I didn't come up with a viable plan so my feelings would become obvious to everyone. Then the thought came to me that I alone would be no match but if I could persuade others to join me in my quest, we could overtake him by sheer numbers and then I could take my rightful place at the helm, it shouldn't be that difficult building an army from the angels at hand because for the most part they're use to taking orders, very few make their own decisions and even then that decision is based on leadership, I just have to convince them that my quest is best for all. But little did I know how loyal that even the seemingly mindless beings were to their lord and master, even with the superior mind that I possess it took eons more to get a rise out of any of them, but slowly my reasoning began to sink in, very slowly, I knew that even at this point although my plan had some merit the chance of me building an army great enough to defeat the almighty out right was very slim, there was just too many of them with absolute loyalty. So I added a new element to my original plan, trickery, the only chance I had of persuading these creatures on a larger scale would be by disregarding the truth and resulting to false accusations, filling their minds with illusions of the truth, it will still be a long shot because obviously these beings have a lot more sense than I first thought, but my mind is still superior to theirs so I'm thinking I can make this happen, and I'm also thinking that even though it is a long shot, it's my only one, I am not a being to be summoned, I have the capacity to rule all, and I will rule all. Then the next time the angels were gathered I seized the opportunity to instill false yet very convincing messages into their minds, with each one knowing in their hearts that they were not true but my presentation was overwhelming, I was very persistent and unyielding, then without them having a chance to gather their own thoughts some began to succumb and more followed suit as the gatherings began to increase, finally my plan was beginning to feel attainable, I finally had an army, a very sizable force of powerful beings ready at my command to take on the creator himself, but maybe I should wait because I feel I can double, even triple the size of our might, but my patience is at the end, one more summons and I'm going to lose all control, one more summons and I'll attack the most high myself, so the onslaught has to be at once and since he won't be expecting us we will take him before he has a chance to respond. So I assembled my army quickly and commanded them to silence, then I went over my plans down to the tiniest detail, instilling the importance of surprise,'let's go and claim our kingdom'I told them in a whisper, then turned and led them to the throne of the creator of existence. Though my army's intentions were to arrive in a silent mode, our steps were amplified as we drew nearer to the throne, in fact the closer we got the louder our steps became until the sound was deafening, what started out to be a sneak attack was now a spectacle. The most high sat in silence, surrounded by all of the remaining residents in his kingdom, so I signaled my army to stop their advancement and we just stood motionless, for a short time it was absolutely quiet, an eerie silence that made me realize how fruitless this mission was and now waiting for the most high to speak and bracing to see the side of him that I've never seen before, his wrath,'sire'I started to speak,'silence'the almighty demanded, it was then that I felt my vocal cords literary dissolve, my voice was gone, I no longer had the ability to speak, then a feeling of complete helplessness overshadow me, feared gripped my whole being, I knew then that my punishment was going to be very severe, suddenly I longed for my former life, the summons, the entertainment, the joy I use to see in the most high eyes, the smile on his face that lit up eternity itself, and now I couldn't even look him in the face, my betrayal was reason for absolute separation, but I was right about one thing that even in an endless kingdom, there's only room for one king, one absolute ruler, and now it was without any doubt the most high, my thoughts were interrupted as the exalted one spoke,'Satan I've monitored your actions since your beginning, I sensed your displeasure, I had hoped that by leaving you alone you would somehow come to your senses, you have disappointed me, you labeled me a tyrant, a ruler with no regard for any of you, so be it, I created you all for my entertainment, to worship me and only me, yet to do so with joy not malice, so for your betrayal you will never again enjoy the pleasures of my kingdom, I will greatly increase your punishment, but for now I want you out of my presence',then the creator focus his attention on my now depleted army and said'you were all a special part of me so that makes your betrayal unforgivable, you will be banished as well'then the most high turned his attention to his archangel and said,'remove them all from my presence and see that their return be monitored at all times' so Micheal directed his army to remove us from not only the presence of the most high but we were thrown out of the kingdom itself.

The kingdom, our home since becoming a part of existence, now it was replaced by a very tiny planet called earth, this was a disgrace, I was intimidated to the point of humiliation, I Satan once considered supreme among the angels top entertainer to the most high God, banished to a world where mere mammals dwelled, and then as if that wasn't enough now I have to deal with the anger of the angels that's stuck here because of me. Unless I think of an alternative plan very quickly things are about to get chaotic, the powerful army I had assembled to unseat the creator was all joining forces and I was the target of their wrath, so my mind immediately went to work because my survival was at stake and due to the failure of the previous one this plan had to be flawless,'listen to me'I found myself shouting,'sure we've been exiled but this gives us a chance to regroup, to correct the wrongs, we couldn't defeat the creator among ourselves but now we dwell in a world with creatures he made after his likeness, so if they are like him then we'll build an army of them to fight alone with us, we can't possible lose with a force of creatures as wise and as powerful as the creator himself'once my speech was finished I braced for the onslaught of a multitude of angry fallen angels just in case it had been ineffective, but it worked, the new plan sunk in somehow, penetrating the senses of this enrage mob, at first only a few but eventually they all agreed to give it a try, I don't know if it was the speech itself or did the feeling that there was little else that could be done that was the convincing factor, either way now came the hard part of actually converting these beings to our point of view. All they know is the creator, his word is law, getting them to betray him might be a lot harder than it was to convert the angels, one thing for sure is they're not going to accept me in my present state, so for this plan to work it's going to take trickery, deception, straight out lies, for this plan to work I can't have a conscious, I can't care about anybody or anything, from now on nothing is off limits, the most high discarded me as scum, but there will be another battle, a much greater one when I will finally dethrone him and he will bow before me, then the universe itself will be my domain and the archangel will pay for his treachery. Hmm the man seem strong defiant, but the woman seem a little more flexible with a certain amount of curiosity that I may be able to exploit, she spends a lot of time gazing at the fruits on that tree, I'll start with her but I need to look less threatening but convincing, I'll have to possess something but what, I see birds flying in and out of that tree, maybe I'll, no they don't look firm enough, the monkeys that's it, I'll take control of a monkey then persuade her to eat the fruit, this has to work because it may be my only chance, okay I'm in now to seduce her, I'm trying but his attention span is creating a huge problem, there's too many of them distracting him, well that was a wasted effort, I've got to find the right subject to possess but there's so many of them, animals, fowls, insects, none of them fit, maybe I'll just hmm that reptile has a interesting form, it's firm, traveling alone which means no distractions and I think it will somehow get the woman's full attention, it will have to do. I've got him phase one of my plan is about to begin, as I neared the woman I said matter of factly,'the fruits on this tree are very exquisite, like no others in the garden, they look extremely tasty why don't you try one'but the woman replied'they are a delight to the eyes but the most high forbid it, he said that they have a special quality besides their beauty, as I understand if eaten they possess the power of death'then I said'do you really believe that look at them, how could something that pleasing to the eyes cause such tragedy, let me tell you a little secret, the most high know that if you eat that fruit it will give you substantial knowledge, you will no longer be servants, but you will be as wise as he is, you will be able to make your own decisions, live the way you want to live, now look at them again, doesn't what I just told you seem more logical than a catastrophic death,'after finishing my speech I studied the woman's facial expression, at first I saw confusion, but then she reached up and grabbed one of the fruits from the tree and just held it in her hand, gazing at it as if hypnotized, then she placed it to her mouth and took a small bite,'hmm this is good'she said and took another bite, the man stood spellbound as if he was waiting for the earth to open and swallow them both, but nothing happened, then she turned to the man and gave him the partially eaten fruit, since there was no change that he was aware of he tasted it himself and life as they knew it changed forever. Now I had one victory against the creator and it couldn't have happened at a better time, because after the fallen angels saw what happened in the garden it gave them reasonable hope that we could eventually overcome the enormous odds against us and emerge absolute, but just as important is it gave me time. So at our next gathering we discussed in detail sinister ways to fulfill our missions, our former way of doing things put to many limitations on our actions, if we're going to have a viable chance when the final battle began we have to be relentless, no rules, no remorse, I learned another phase of deception that day and I know that there's so much more to learn, because these earth dwelling creatures are not all alike as I look for my next victim I swell with anticipation and I have a very good feeling that the woman will be my most powerful weapon, and she was, as the earth grew in population she became irreplaceable. I used her beauty and her body to cause the creators most powerful men to fall, her flattering words were irresistible, all men succumb to her, she is a force to be exonerated because of nature itself.

Through the ages the victories mounted to such an extreme degree that the world the creator had designed for his amusement became a foul evil place, my army and I worked relentlessly to corrupt all life, the earth had now become a dark planet with only a few remaining loyal to the most high, my plan was now in full effect so I figured it would only be a matter of time before man will do my bidding. I'm getting stronger and wiser, once I take complete control of all life I will challenge the most high again, wait I can hardly believe what's taking place, I would recognize him anywhere, he's actually going through with it, I've got to gather my army at once this could change everything,'listen all of you, everything is going as planned, we have mankind in our service and the big news is we've been presented with a very generous gift, the creator has made it easy for us, he has taken on the form of flesh and is presently here on earth, so since he has stepped into time then all the rules that govern humankind apply to him as well and that means he is under the power of the death angel, now if death claims him we will not only rule this world but we can assault the great kingdom itself, without the power of the most high to sustain it we will conquer and rule with no mercy, then I will finally take my rightful place upon the throne'I listened as the cheers and applause began, then as I looked over the multitude of fallen angels I saw joy on each of their faces as they realized that this tireless battle was finally about to pay off, that our war against the creator was at the end with us as victors. Yes the moment of truth was at hand and we knew that at all cost the most high couldn't be allowed to return to the great kingdom, from the time he was born we launched an all out assault, attempting to kill him by any means, trying to freeze him making sure there were no warm rooms available, but the manger his parents found depleted that plan, so I tricked the king into thinking that the baby was born to take his place thinking that plan would surely be foolproof, but I didn't anticipate the angel Gabriel's warning causing him to escape death's grip again and that's when I first realized that this was going to be a lot harder than I thought. So I decided that since he still had divine help that I would attack his humanity, he had taken on flesh and flesh had certain needs, so those needs is what I began focusing on, bombarding him with one temptation after another, but he would not succumb needless to say I began to worry because if he could overtake me in his weakest state how could I hope to defeat him at all, but I couldn't give up, everything depended on my finding a way to stop him. Attacking him directly just wasn't working so a indirect approach was my only remaining hope and of course that meant employing the creatures he had once been so proud of, mankind, my trickery was still very much effective although he was undermining a lot of the progress I had made by being an example as to how the type of life he demanded from these servants could actually be accomplished, he's upsetting the whole flow of the order in which I had things, he's a more dangerous threat as a man than he was as a God, he's got to be silenced and he's got to be silenced at once. I tried to have him stoned but he escaped, it was as if he was untouchable, then the idea came to me that he has a hedge around him, devoted followers providing him protection, I must disrupt his security, I've got to get someone he trust to betray his loyalty, then I can stop his onslaught and preserve a chance of winning this war. So I observed all of his followers and to my dismay they appeared undeterred, is nothing simple, must everything be so complicated, I'll assign a platoon to watch them with the urgency of reporting any weakness at once, we don't have a moment to spare, so I assigned seven angels to each one of them with special instructions of never ending enticements, through the years the flesh has proven to be more of a liability than asset so it shouldn't take long to get one or more of them to fall to temptation and once that happens it will only be a matter of time before the most high mission here on earth comes to an end. Then as if on cue we overpowered one of his followers with of course trickery and deception, then without hesitation my troops pounced on the situation giving way to the opening of the untouchable hedge in which the most high had surrounded himself. Now I can end this madness, so I gathered all of my most notable servants and prepared their minds for the death of the Christ, nothing short of that will do and sure enough before long the Christ was giving up his ghost, at last we stood victorious, the Messiah was firmly in the grip of the death angel and without that added power the most high was weakened. Now the greatest battle of all lied ahead, the one that will end this war permanently, and change the whole course of existence, the one that will bring the most high to his knees'hear me my strong and faithful followers, we have defeated the Christ and now we must prepare to take on the most high himself, with his defeat we will own existence, then we will have an eternity to celebrate, until that time do not lose focus of our ultimate goal'as I ended my speech I noticed it did nothing to stop the celebration my troops had begun already, they were ecstatic, all remembering how the Christ had been the major factor in our banishment from the great kingdom, so looking at his lifeless body, not to mention the totally abusive way in which his demise came to be, brought on a satisfaction never before experienced. I am not without the desire of letting my guards down as well after all of the eons of combat but I know we have to press forward, especially now that we have the upper hand, the creator is nobody's fool, he has to have a backup plan and that is what worries me. Before long the creator's backup plan revealed itself in a way that shattered all of our hopes, the Christ broke death's grip and picked up his life, but not just the life he gave up as a man but the life he gave up as a God as well, with enough power to bring all of earth and beyond to it's knees, I knew it, now the most high not only enhanced his grip on all that lives but all that dies as well, how can I ever expect to defeat the almighty, now just the thought of his power send chills through my being, but I can't give up because we have no choice in the matter, we're doomed without mercy so we have to continue this fight even with the feeling of hopelessness. I have to rally my troops, bring them out of the shocked state that's overwhelmed them all, there's power emitting throughout the universe, radiating every fiber of existence, so I have to think quickly, there has to be some way to motivate my army, but what can I tell them that sounds believable even to me

The things that started to affect my thoughts didn't help matters at all, I thought back to how this war had begun, the role I had in the great kingdom, thinking it was beneath me, but now it would be very appreciated, what was I thinking, how could I have been so stupid thinking I could be like the most high, maybe if I went to him and kneeled begging for his mercy, he will have compassion, even if I couldn't get my honor role again surely some lowly position would be attainable, but even as I was entertaining the thought I knew it would never happen, the damage was much too vast to erase the seriousness of it. Because of me the future of man has been altered, because of me the Christ suffered unmercifully and now that he has emerged what makes me think I can just throw in the towel and all be forgiven, I've got to overcome this feeling and regain my composure, we've got to win this war, the creator has one weakness mankind, if there is any chance of my victory that is where it lies, I've got to keep exploiting them until enough of them forsake him and join us, that will be my motivation speech, I will summon my army and give them a ray of hope, I won't have to explain the urgency because we're all aware of that. Then on one accord we set out to turn the creator's most prize creation against him, every weapon at our disposal was used persistently, the earth became a very violent and inhumane world and the ones who remained loyal to the creator were being stamp out at a very rapid pace, our mission was going very well, most of them was easily persuaded, others more intense tactics proved successful, none of us knew when that great day would come, the day when the most high would call all into his presence, but we did know that when it came we would need all of the help we could get. These creatures were advancing dangerously, the arsenal they had accumulated would be very useful, in fact with all of their scientific technology I began to see why they were considered to be like God himself, their combine brain power was astonishing and the more powerful they became the more they dismiss the creator, this was working out better than I could ever have thought possible, this renewed my hope, my confidence, I even saw motivation among my troops again, the fire in their eyes had returned, we believed we actually had a chance at victory again. For some reason the most high was delaying the great day which gave us time to get stronger, then I began to think that the delay was because he knew how powerful we were, maybe he wasn't sure he could defeat us now and didn't want to risk it, maybe he will dismiss it indefinitely being content to rule the great kingdom only while I rule this world and the one below. Well whatever the reason for his delay benefits my purpose, because once my power is sufficient I want be satisfied with just this tiny planet and the underworld, I'll insist on ruling the universe itself, all existence will be mine to command, I won't stop until the most high and his Christ fall to their knees before me, then I will be king of kings and lord of lords'my loyal and faithful troops hear my voice, I stand before you as I did from the beginning, we have become a very powerful force of one, the most high feel our might all the way from his throne which will soon be my throne, then all will call me King Satan, now go there is still much to be done for the great day is getting nearer and we must be ready'then I watched as my army dispersed, each of them knowing their mission, each more motivated than ever to execute every opportunity, all of them knowing without a doubt the urgency every passing moment bring. I will join them in our quest but first I must make sure every detail of the plans I have arranged for that day is carried out without fail and now after reviewing my victory strategy I feel it is without blemish, I no longer fear the most high in fact I feel superior, I'm looking forward to the great day because I control an army as vast as the sands of the sea'hear me creator and hear me well, I feel endowed enough to appoint the great day myself, I will come for the great kingdom and I will come without mercy'as I shouted these words I believed them immensely, I felt unstoppable, why should I wait on the most high when I can take the fight to him. So I gathered all of the forces at my command, spirits and flesh, then I had them ignite the most powerful weapons in their arsenal, weapons with enough power to destroy all life on this planet and beyond, now we're a force to be reckon with, a force to be feared, I felt invincible, the time had come to take the battle to the great kingdom. But before I realize what was happening the universe became silent, a unfamiliar eerie silence, light vanished as if it never existed, the vast cold emptiness of space was suddenly heated profusely and then the bang, a bang that caused all matter to dissipate, and then there was nothing, no stars, no suns, no planets, no galaxies, it was as if existence just ceased to be, then I saw a sight that left me speechless, thoughtless, motionless, deprived of any will at all, a sight that left no doubt at all as to who was in total control, a sight that sent the vast army that I had accumulated scattering, attempting to find any escape route, but there was none, all weapons were useless as we stood before the great throne of the most high God, we then went from standing to kneeling I knew this was it, I had looked forward to this day somehow thinking I would be the victor, but realizing at this moment that I never had a chance, how can such power be equaled, how can the creation possible defeat the creator, how could I have thought that partial might could uproot all might, just then I saw all the troops I once commanded fate sealed as they became eternally banished to their punishment, now I alone remained, bracing for the punishment I knew was about to be thrust upon me, and then as I was being banished myself my last sane remark was 'I am King Satan'.

The Rollercoaster Ride to the Unknown

written by Rocky Earl Smith-a.k.a. Darkbrain

The renovation turned out to be a success, Bob was glad he had followed through with his plans because at first glance of the once thriving then totally depleted amusement park had more than once prompted him to abort the mission, the whole area was a disaster, a real dinosaur of a landscape. But Bob took on the challenge anyway, giving it his full focus, and now as he traveled around observing the improvements of his finished recreation, he was glad he had persevered, the place was first class, it had cost him and his partners a major fortune but he figured it was a small price to pay for the return this investment was sure to make them. Anyway now that the project was complete the grand opening he had planned would be a grand slam, Bob planned on opening the amusement park with discounts on every ride, hopefully drawing in a huge crowd to start things off, then after the customers were enticed, he was sure that word of mouth would bring more of them, not to mention repeaters, yes he was very confident that this new business adventure was the one that would put him on the map. And sure enough when the amusement park opened there was standing room only, the people of Superior, Idaho didn't have a lot of recreational resorts so this was like an answer to their prayers, they cram into the resort spending lots and lots of money and of course that made Bob ecstatic, he had spared no expense and now it was coming back in record time, every ride in the park was redesign to perfection but the highlight of this new found gold mine was the rollercoaster. It was unique, state of the arts, it not only did the norm but it excelled, reaching speeds that would have been considered extremely dangerous by most standards, but with the new technology Bob had incorporated it was now considered a thrill, the public couldn't get enough, but as with most new technology sometimes there are major risks and this one was no exception as the Rusk family was about to experience. Bill and Susan, along with their three children, William Jr, Dolly, and Peter could hardly wait to ride the new thrill seeker, the excitement was bubbling over, and as Bill was giving the attendant the tickets, Susan had her hands full trying to control their children, this situation continued as they all got onto the roller coaster and was strapped in, in fact everyone on the ride was so excited that containment was an issue, then after making sure everyone was secure the attendant press the start button as cheers echoed through the crowd. Then as the Roller coaster began it's journey, screams of excitement was heard by children as well as the adults as the speed became faster and faster, with the excitement only growing as the spellbinding ride soared, but no one could have anticipated what was about to take place. For most of the patrons things went on without a hitch, but for a selected few not so much and the Rusk family was soon to learn their fate as the roller coaster came to a gradual stop, it was very apparent to not only Bill and Susan, but to their three kids as well that something was amiss, once they came to a complete stop the five of them looked around in bewilderment at the scene that was displayed before them, none of them knew what had taken place but all of them knew that this didn't look like Superior Idaho anymore. The scene they beheld was a wasteland, everything they saw was barren, the trees were dried to their roots, it was a wonder that they was still standing, there was no grass at all only swampland, there were no buildings, no structure of any type and then there was the eerie silence, no fowl, no animals, no insects, and the most disturbing part of all was no humans, it was as if they had entered another dimension, another realm if you will, an aftermath of some sort or God forbid an before the status quota, either way the whole scenario was creeping them all out and soon the children began asking questions the parents couldn't answer. Dolly started crying telling them she was scared and wanted to go home, with Peter soon following suit, William Jr by being the oldest tried very hard to be brave but soon cave in to his fears and began crying as well, even though Bill and Susan attempted to console their children, they knew it was fruitless because they were on edge and astoundly confused themselves, not to mention the enormous fear that had gripped them as well, it was like they were all in a nightmare and had landed in another world. Susan tried for the kids sake to keep herself intact but soon Bill was the only member of the family with dry eyes, this situation was catastrophic but Bill knew that if he caved it would lead to a total disaster and he couldn't allow that to happen to his family, but of course it wasn't easy as question after question bombarded his mind, question like where the hell are we? How did we get here? Is there a way back? Are there other people somewhere in this God forsaken place?where do we go from here?how am I going to feed my family?and why did this have to happen to us?with so many unanswered questions and the constant interruptions by his panic stricken family, Bill found himself barely maintaining his sanity, as the manager of his firm he was used to stressful predicaments and growing up as the eldest of four siblings the leadership roll pretty much came with the territory, but this situation wasn't normal, how can a person prepare for an event that hinges on the supernatural, but be that as it may this is the hand he was dealt so for he and his family's sake his actions had to be flawless, the least mistake could cause their demise, then he ordered his family to follow him and stay as close as possible, as he tried to lead his family to safety Bill looked in every direction very carefully, scoping the entire grounds, the surrounding objects, nothing went unnoticed, but he couldn't help thinking to himself that the situation was hopeless, that he and his love ones would die here, but despite of that very depressing thought Bill led and his family followed.

He led them as carefully as possible through the barren wasteland instructing them not to touch anything not knowing what type of contamination the debris possess, they traveled about fifty yards through lifeless swamp water, his family's crying and complaining was beginning to become unbearable, so much so that Bill just wanted to take off running and screaming himself, his head was pounding, his body and feet hurt, his stomach was growling unmerciful, but his thirst actually triumph everything else, the real pain was realizing that if he was suffering to this extreme, his family had every right to complain. He didn't know how but he did know that for them to avoid tragedy he had to feed his wife and kids, and soon which cause him to experience an anxiety attack, compounded with the rest of his ailments led to a heart attack, no Bill thought not now, this can't be happening, I've got to beat this for the sake of my family, but the pain was too intense, leveling him and taking him to the ground. Susan saw the pain in her husband's eyes and the grimace on his face, then heard herself screaming realizing what was taking place, she immediately kneeled beside Bill administering C.P.R. and pounding his chest trying frantically to retrieve a heartbeat, she continued to try to save her husband while the children wailed and screamed uncontrollable, Bill's last thought was please God take care of my family, then he was gone, but Susan didn't give up trying to revive him in fact she continued until exhaustion demanded that she stop, then still kneeling beside Bill's lifeless body in a total state of shock tears blinded her, her eyes could see nothing, but her ears and the rest of her senses told her that the kids needed her desperately, she knew that somewhere within her she had to draw the strength to stop being a widow and assume her role as a mother. Little Dolly was drenched, her face was as red as crimson, her eyes were swollen to the point of closure and she had pee on herself, little Peter wasn't doing much better, he had basically the same symptoms except he had completely relieved himself, Susan knew she had to find them both something to change into otherwise they would both have to travel without their undies and pants to avoid getting chapped. Then there was William Jr who after witnessing his father's death become zombie like, emotionless, expressionless, immobile, he just continued to stare at his father's corpse in total confusion, this had gone from one of the most exciting days in his young life to the most horrific one, they had gotten up that morning anticipating the day ahead, his father told them the news the night before, William Jr found it hard to sleep that night due to his excitement, every since the amusement park had opened he and his siblings had looked forward to the day when their parents was going to take them, they had past it numerous times and each time it looked more and more exciting, on the drive to the park that morning his head was filled with visions of the rides, the food, the contests, by all accounts this was going to be a day to remember, a day he would return and brag to his friends about, but now with them God knows where and him standing looking down at his father, his hero, knowing his idol would not be returning home with them, tears began rolling down his face but only for a moment because he knew his mother needed him now that his father was gone, so even though he was too young to fully understand the concept little William Jr began to man up, now he was able to turn his focus from his father's blue decaying body unto his mother. Susan was moving on adrenaline only, she was way passed exhaustion, the only thing keeping her going was her children, if not for them she would surely lay down next to her deceased husband and pray for death, but she had to persevere because she was now the head of the family, no longer could she seek the solace of her husband's security and this was a role she was not accustomed to, Susan had been pampered all of her life, by her being the only child her parents gave her everything she wanted, and then she met Bill who continued the tradition so to suddenly be dealt a hand of this magnitude was really flipping her out but for the sake of her kids she drew on strength she had no idea was in her. She began with little Dolly removing her shorts and undies, she then turned her attention to little Peter repeating the same actions, but since he had soiled himself as well she used his shorts to clean him, and once she had finish her little ones began to calm down somewhat, but she figured it was because they were all cried out so she turned her attention to her eldest child but wasn't quite prepared for what she beheld, he wasn't crying, wasn't showing no signs of fear, in fact for a brief moment Susan could see his father in his small form. William Jr's behavior sent out an aura that helped his mother regain her composure, even though he was only nine years old he held his head up high and helped his mother with his smaller siblings, Susan didn't want to leave Bill's body unprotected even though there was no wildlife present, she didn't trust this world they had suddenly been forced to try to survive in, so with the help of William Jr she covered her husband's body as best as she could and then she looked in every direction trying to decide the safest path to take, a path that she hoped would not only lead to food but to civilization as well she knew her family really needed food and water to live, but as she looked around she noticed that all the paths were exact duplicates of the others, barren, eerie, lifeless, then confusion overtook her again, but this time William Jr seeing his mother in disarray came to her aid and suggested a direction for them to take, then he grab little Peter's hand while Susan took little Dolly's hand out of reflex and the four of them proceeded in the direction her son had pointed out, thankfully there was no wildlife in the swamps. After they had traveled about fifty yards they all stood in awe of the transformation that had taken place right before their eyes, the barren wasteland was now a paradise, every tree was now flowing with different fruits, the grass was richly green, food spring up in the form of vegetables, watermelons, grapes, sugar canes, with wildlife roaming plentifully, fowl, animals, enough meat to sustain them for a lifetime although Susan had no plans of spending anymore time in this mysterious world than she had to, her focus was on getting her family back to their home in Superior Idaho, but she was very thankful to be in this land of milk and honey as opposed to that God forsaken barren wasteland they had just emerged from. And as she was picking fruits from the trees and handing them to her children she marveled at how close but totally different the two worlds were, then as she took a bite out of a fruit herself she remembered it had been a short distance of about fifty yards that she and her husband had taken with their children to begin with that had landed them in that wasteland where Bob had collapsed, then an eerie feeling came over her as she looked around for water so she and her kids could wet their bellies, all of their throats were very dry, but thankfully she didn't have to look far, there was water everywhere in the form of rivers, streams, waterfalls, so she led her three children to one of the smaller streams so she could not only let them drink but bathe them as well. Susan was undeniable relieved that she and her kids was full and clean, so now while little Dolly and Peter's clothing was drying this temporary fulfillment gave her mind time to reflect, her thoughts immediately remembered Bob, his lifeless body lying not fifty yards from her in that swampland was deeply depressing, but she reasoned that it was the safest place to keep it for the time being, at least until she could figure out a way to get home, home the thought of it sent her mind into a whirl spin, she began thinking of their modest really nice house, the bedroom that she shared with her husband, then next to it was little Dolly's room, with the little ponies on the wallpaper, and a wide assortment of dolls that even Susan herself played with very often even though she owned quite a few herself, then there was the boys bedroom with their bunk beds and ninja turtles wallpaper, William Jr was always protected of his little brother who just turned seven, and the both of them guarded Dolly, who was five, then Susan's mind continued the journey through the family home starting with the bathroom, the kitchen, the den, the library, onto the two car garage, and then ending with the backyard and it's contents, the patio, the swimming pool slash jacuzzi, not to mention the tamperine, it was so hard to believe all of this had happen in such a short time, they were just there not four hours ago. Susan wish that she had never seen the amusement park especially the r oller coaster that was the point of entry what if they went back to that point and waited, maybe at a particular time it would again arrive at that spot then they could ride it back to their world, that was the only logical solution, it would certainly beat wondering around in this seemingly endless changing world, so she relayed her plan to William Jr because she would need his help to fulfill a very important part of it, to help carry her husband's body to the point of entry.

Susan hoped that once she got back to their home they could at least give Bill a proper burial, so she told her children to eat and drink as much as possible because she had no idea how long it would take for them to get back to their world, but she had to think in a positive mode, there was too much at stake for her plan not to work. So after dressing little Peter and Dolly she looked in the direction of the barren wasteland from which they had come, thinking that just fifty yards from that swamp filled nothingness this nightmare should come to an end, then she grabbed little Dolly's hand as William Jr grabbed little Peter's and began the short journey, but anxiety brought Susan's mind to a halt, she tried very hard to contain this rush but it became too much and the pressure stopped Susan's heart, her last thoughts were please God take care of my children, then she was gone. Little Dolly was at her mother's side trying to awake her, with little Peter joining in the quest, they both screamed very loudly over and over for their mother to open her eyes and when she didn't they started to cry, William Jr watched as his mother took her last breath, then immediately his mind reflected to a short time earlier when his father did the same, now they were all alone in this strange world, but he remembered his mother's plan and was determined to carry it out, it was her last request. So without thinking the nine year old took his two siblings by their hand and proceeded toward the area where the roller coaster had dropped them off, it wasn't easy because his little sister and brother was resisting, screaming for their mother, but he was persistence and continued to pull them toward their destination, it took what seemed like hours to cover the fifty yards to the place where their father had collapsed and even longer to travel the remaining fifty yards to the point of entry, but he guided the two without hesitation until they finally reached the designated spot, needless to say William Jr was exhausted, his two smaller siblings was barely controllable and to top it off there was no sign of the big machine that had brought them here, in fact there was no sign that it had ever been there. he was so disappointed that he joined his little brother and sister and started crying, they were all alone and scared, their parents had died right in front of them, none of them knew what to do next so they hug each other and just continued to cry, this went on for awhile until they suddenly heard a loud noise, a loud familiar sound, then as the three children looked around they all beheld the roller coaster as it came to a stop, then without any hesitation they ran toward the huge glowing machine, the lock handle was already ajar and waiting as William Jr helped Dolly onto the platform first, followed closely by his little brother Peter and then hopping aboard himself, once they were all seated the handle lock secured itself. The three waited in anticipation, but the great machine remained motionless, the children didn't know what to do next so they just sat there, hoping that the roller coaster would start moving, then as time passed the kids became restless not understanding why the big machine wouldn't move, how could they know that this thrill rider with all of it's technology sensed two vacant spots in it's interior and was waiting for them to be filled, but after hours of delay the great machine signals became crossed, because when the children had gotten restless they began moving all over the inside of the seats causing the signals to malfunction, but the children were not just disrupting the machines sensors, you see while the three little ones was moving about they were frantically calling for their parents, it was like the past few hours of chaos was wiped completely from their young memories and each one of them as if on cue screamed at the top of their voice without cease, mama, daddy, the roller coaster was used to kids and adults alike hollering and screaming from excitement and from fear, but the screams of these three children was somehow different, so the great machine's sensors not only malfunction, but was overcome with confusion as the backup sensors kicked in, and once the backup was in full operation the thrill ride took off leaving the world of the unknown behind, traveling the remaining distance of the amusement park, which was you guessed it about fifty yards, as it approached the starting gate it came to a complete stop. The attendant greeted the Rusk family with a smile on his face as they exited the great machine'was your experience satisfactory sir?' He ask'yes it was like nothing I've ever enjoyed, it was quite an adventure'Bill answered him as he assisted his wife and three children off the thrill ride, after the children were unloaded they began running toward the next one, with Susan trying to keep up and screaming at them to be careful with Bill in close pursuit, meanwhile the attendant still smiling greeted the next thrill riders, loaded them up and started the roller coaster on to it's next journey into the unknown.

The Spirit of Life

written by Rocky Earl Smith-a.k.a. darkbrain

The earth smoothly spins at a constant pace, sending powerful magnetic forces into empty space

The sunlight descend casting radiating rays, evaporating water vapors into energy filled days

The rain falls downward moisturizing below, filling oceans, filling rivers giving streams full flow

These are some of the events in the hemisphere, when the spirit of life soars through the atmosphere

Energy flows transforming life to all kind, signaling all the wonders of nature to rise in due time

Powerful energetic vibes are there to enforce, and ensure that the creator's will remain on course

Death takes it's vacation during these chain of events, and remain off for a season time well spent

So there's no resistance in the hemisphere, when the spirit of life soars through the atmosphere

There's life in the air the soil the water, new life in mammals the animals all matter

Atoms congregating as one to make a whole, creating new bodies new minds new souls

Yes death is dismissed this time of the year, when the spirit of life soars through the atmosphere

The Unlimited Mind

written by\Rocky Earl Smith

My eyes see the beauty of woman so pure, my mind see the makings of a potential wife

My eyes see the wonders designed by nature, my mind see the works of supreme life

My eyes see that people are basically good, my mind see the transgression within

My ears hear so many things misunderstood, my mind hear the true message it sends

My body feel the stress of human fate, my mind sense the vibes of blasphemy

My ears hear the sound of so much hate, my mind hear the voice of jealousy

My mind deals with total reality, my mind is a part of everything

My mind stay focus on the real enemy, my mind reigns supreme

The Legend of the Ice Cream Vendor Murders

written by Rocky Earl Smith\a.k.a. darkbrain

The music was loud and joyous, echoing through the airwaves like a soothing melody of excitement, the neighborhood children danced and played in anticipation of soon seeing the ice cream vendor coming down the street, visions of multi colored cool delights going round and around in their heads, even the adults were waiting along the sidewalks laughing and joking, but trying to keep some form of adulthood about them when deep inside they just wanted to release all inhibitions and act like children themselves. As the music grew louder they could all see the ice cream vendor's truck turning onto their street and slowly coming toward them, their excitement grew as the truck neared but soon their excitement turned to confusion when the truck stopped for none of them but kept it's gradual pace moving down the street stopping only once it reached the stop sign at the corner, there it just remained which by now some of the people had gotten a little upset but others noted that during the course of it's slow journey pass them the ice cream vendor was not visible so in concern they proceeded to where the truck had stopped not knowing what they would find but knowing something wasn't right and after looking inside sure enough the vendor appeared to be dead. Their first thought was that he had had a heart attack, some of them rushed into the truck to see if they could be of any help while others called nine one-one reporting the emergency, before long emergency responders were on the scene because they were stationed in the neighborhood, but even if they had been on the spot it wouldn't have help the ice cream vendor because it would soon be discovered that he had been dead for a while and not from a heart attack as was first expected, but from bullet wounds, yes the ice cream vendor had been murdered, shot straight in the head and through his heart, the truck immediately became a crime scene, all fingerprints lifted from the surface of the truck was matched to the owners and interviews with those people were set up but later cleared. The neighborhood was canvass with investigators looking for any leads, spent bullet shells, blood spilled on the ground, any suspicious scenario nothing would be dismissed, neighbors were questioned constantly with police observing very closely how each of them reacted, but no leads were found, the news headline said'friendly neighborhood ice cream vendor murdered'police seeked the public's help but to no avail. The next day the mystery took on new meaning when another ice cream vendor was found murdered inside of his truck, the same procedures were implemented and the same results were concluded, but by the two men being killed in the same way it became apparent that the same person had shot them both, so the police gave the killer a name'the ice cream man slayer'and a reward of twenty-five thousand dollars was offered to anyone who could lead authorities to an arrest and conviction. Leads came in by the thousands all of them checked, but none of them exposed the killer, so police presence increased in the more influentially neighborhoods while the less fortunate zip codes were left to fend for themselves and that was where the murders were taking place. Case in point was the next ice cream vendor murder, it seemed the killer wanted to make a statement because even though it was the same m.o. as far as the shot in the head, it was different because of the caliber of the weapon, this ice cream vendor's head was completely removed from it's torso by a multi pellet shotgun, the crime scene was a total mess luckily no children had seen the bodies of any of the slain, especially this one, they only knew that their friendly ever smiling ice cream man had been murdered and just that knowledge alone gave some of them nightmares and left all of them feeling fear when they heard that formally joyous music coming from the most popular truck in the neighborhood. The ice cream vendors that remained took a deep cut in profits, that compounded with not knowing if a potential sell would lead to their murder was enough to drive some of them out of the business while others hired people to ride with them to stand guard against potential danger, because even with the cut in profits due to widespread fear the selling of ice cream during these very heated days was still a lucrative business and that paid a lot of bills, for that reason and that reason alone there were those who was not going to be deterred from doing what they do best. Some even tried to form some sort of union figuring their was safety in numbers, so with all of the unity some time passed before another tragedy took place, but when it did it made the previous ones look mediocre, case in point, one very hot and muggy afternoon, an idea time for selling those multi colored cold refreshments, tragedy happened, as usual there were rows of people children and adults, each one mouth watering with anticipated taste buds, all of them ready to pounce upon the truck and begin ordering their cool delights, then as if right on cue the ice cream truck came rolling down the street it's music blaring to capacity, this time it was like the previous tragedies with one huge exception, the truck didn't stop and this time people didn't have to wait to see why, as the truck passed the crowd could see the occupants, well their heads anyway, the way their eyes bulked and protruded from their sockets left no doubt as to their condition. Screams were heard, children cried hysterically, and again nine one-one was called but this time it was directed to the police department because there was no doubt in anyone's mind that death had visited and claimed the two truck's occupants. The scene was so gruesome that even the coroner had trouble adjusting, the most puzzling part was that at first sight the two bodies appeared to be missing that is until they were later discovered stuffed in the coolers and just like before a full investigation was lunged which in turn brought about a considerable amount of leads, producing no results that is until one particular call came in from what sounded like the voice of a child, according to the voice on the other end of the phone he not only knew who was committing the murders but knew his residence as well and told the police all, opting not to claim the reward which now had risen to fifty thousand dollars, the voice just wanted the killings to stop, he also provided details as to when would be the best time to catch the killers at home. The officers had a hard time grasping the fact that after all of these months of being completely in the dark concerning this case, that just like that it would soon all be over, but preparations were implemented for the take down of these ruthless murderers and the sooner the better. So surveillance was put in motion as detectives watched the address supplied to them by the informant, at first it appeared to be a host, the people at that residence appeared to be a normal everyday law abiding family of five, consisting of a mother who fit the soccer mom's image to the tiniest detail, then there was the dad who seemed like the typical executive workaholic no family should be without and then there were two girls, the older one looked high school while the younger one looked elementary, then last but not least there was a boy, who appeared to be about thirteen or fourteen, but nothing unusual stood out about him either,'we've been had'one of the detectives told the other,'yes it looks like it'the other one acknowledged 'but let's make one more day out of it since we're already here'when their relief arrived it was already common knowledge that it was going to be an very uneventful shift, but before the torch was passed an unfamiliar truck pulled up to the house in question then the dad came out and got in with the man who was driving and without even looking around to see if they were being watched the two set in the truck talking for what seem like hours, which wasn't out of the ordinary, but what did arouse suspicion was that while the two sat talking a call came into the police headquarters warning them to be on the alert because another killing was about to take place the following morning and the caller was the same one who had called previously giving them the address they now had under surveillance. Once the detectives on duty was relayed the warning and already observing the extensive meeting taking place between the two in the truck suddenly things started to fit, so that knowledge was relayed to the main office and steps were implemented to stop the killers before they could strike again. Finally the dad got out of the truck and went into the house, the reinforcement quad had already arrived on the scene and followed the man in the truck as he pulled off, but the tail didn't last long because his house was right around the corner on the next block, the house he entered was just as nice as the one he'd just left. These were prominent people, very well to do, almost above suspicion, the detectives didn't know as of yet the man's living arrangements but this certainly didn't look like a house a man would buy if he didn't have a family, surveillance was set up at that residence as well for the duration of the night, then right before dawn the man came out and got into his truck and proceeded around the block to pick up the dad and upon seeing this the detectives in both vehicles alerted their superiors and requested instructions as to how to proceed, also seeking backup because they knew something terrible was about to take place and they knew that things had to go right or people was going to die. Orders were given to follow the suspects and as soon as they knew the location of the hit, call so backup could converge on the spot as quickly as possible, the trip took quite a while because the suspects left their side of town and ended up in a more depleted part of the city, a part of the city that simulated where previous hits had taken place, the detectives stayed as far as they could from them without losing sight, but after entering that neighborhood they alerted their superiors and immediately backup was disbursed, but before any help could arrive the two men sprung into action, having located their prey they jumped out of the truck with weapons in hand and headed straight for an ice cream truck that was being prepared for it's daily workout, the detectives seeing what was taking place didn't have time to summarize only to react and instantly the four of them was out of their vehicles heading toward the armed men screaming at them to drop their weapons, telling them they were under arrest, but the suspects paid no attention to them, so they identified themselves again and fired a shot into the air as a warning of what was about to come, after hearing the shot the ice cream vendor ran inside his house for safety and this infuriated the two gunmen who then turned toward the four detectives with vengeance in their eyes, opening fire on them as the detectives returned fire. About that time backup began to arrive and these two men who by just looking at them would think they were model citizens began running toward the officers firing in sequence, it then became apparent that they spent a lot of time at the gun range because of the amount of officers that went down, the investigators finally defused the situation but paid a heavy price in the process, the four detectives who had originally followed them to the crime scene had fallen, along with three of the backup team, seven of the good guys would never see their families again, but as little comfort as it was neither would the killers, the ice cream vendor's truck was riddled with bullet holes and so was his house but at least he would live to work again.

That day the news spread like wildfire, even though it saddened the public to hear of the fallen officers, it gave them back the feeling of security hearing that the ice cream vendor's murderers had been slain, so things went as back to normal as possible considering what had taken place. And now on those sweltering heated days the ice cream vendor's business was in full bloom, soon the past events were just horrible memories until on one particular day the sun was merciless, it was so hot that people's clothes was literary sticking to their bodies, walking the pavement with bare feet actually caused second degree burns, the weatherman was recommending indoor activity because of the strong possibility of heatstroke for even the shortest period in the outdoors, and above all stay hydrated, for the most part people complied, it was a no brainer, but when the sound of that magical music echoed through the airwaves visions of multi colored cold refreshments took over everyone's thoughts and not wanting to miss the treats people lined the sidewalks waiting for the chance to feel that soothing cool sweetness pacifying their insatiable taste buds, yes the mood although hampered by the unnatural heat was subtle, then when the people saw the ice cream truck turn onto their street a loud cheer went out from sheer excitement, but as it got closer the excitement turned to horror when the truck exploded. The scene was horrific as parts of bodies lay everywhere, there was wailing and screaming and hysterical crying from the survivors, but there wasn't many of them, the explosion was so huge that not only the street that the truck was on suffered casualties but the whole neighborhood became a crime scene. The city in fact the nation was in shock as soon as the news hit the airwaves, what had happened, as far as everyone knew the ice cream vendor's killers had been slain, was this the work of a copycat, what would make someone do such a devastating thing, again the public's help was needed because authorities didn't have a clue. It was soon decided to investigate the killers families and extended members along with friends looking for any possibilities, there was of course like in any family tree some very shady characters but none they could link to the crime, at least not yet, so a huge award of one hundred thousand dollars raised by crime stoppers and surviving family members and friends of the murdered. Now authorities could only hope that the amount of the reward would lead to a break in the case, there was a memorial held with love ones pleading for the public's help, people who could bury their family members did and those who didn't have enough of their's left to bury held close caskets memorials. Then about a month after the explosion there was another one, this time the body count wasn't nearly as many but no less tragic, fear took over logic and ice cream vendors were banned for the time being until investigators could get a handle on who was behind all of this disastrous activity, then because of the ban more members of the community joined forces and the reward was raised to two hundred thousand dollars, surely this dollar amount would bring justice to so many who desperately needed it. Investigators first thought was that since the two killers were very influential citizens then there was a strong possibility that whoever bombed the two ice cream trucks were from the same caliber so their focus was on zip codes where people had plenty of resources but not leaving out the fact that it could be any deranged person from any part of the city, undercover officers converged on the streets seeking any reliable informant's information, this was a mystery of the highest proportion, no one had any idea of who was behind these sinister deeds at least no one was talking, and after months of frustration, summer turned to fall and fall to winter, then winter to spring, and now with summer about to resurface it was like the wounds became fresh all over again and a fresh aura of fear circulated throughout the nation, the ban of ice cream trucks remained intact along with a renewed public's outcry for justice, still the two hundred thousand dollar reward led to no significant leads. Then one day well into the summer in fact the date was the fourth of July, a call came into the anonymous tip department, of course there had been numerous false tips, many with hope of claiming the reward, but this call was like none of the others, the voice on the other end was very precise naming detailed information that had been kept from the public, the voice was deep and eerie exhibiting no emotion whatsoever, it was like talking to a dead person, the caller was so informed that it was no way he could be taken for granted, he went on to give names and addresses of where the killers could be found and didn't ask about the reward or any other compensation, then the phone line just went dead, but now investigators had a lead and not just any lead but if the caller's information was accurate it was going to break the case wide open. Then after thinking a minute, they all hoped it wouldn't be like their last break when they lost seven of their comrades, this time a more aggressive yet cautious plan had to be implemented they all know it came with the territory but still the thought of losing more of their friends and coworkers just wasn't a thought any of them wanted to deal with. So surveillance was set up but this time instead of two detectives in a car there were four of them, instead of one car there were three, so all together twelve bullet proof wearing officers were on sight with a host of others on call waiting to converge where ever needed. The house was very luxurious, the occupants this time consisted of multiple family members, in fact it appeared to be more than one family staying in the estate, all of them looked normal in a civilize state of being, but remembering their last encounter with the two killers who looked like perfect citizens brought a sobering mood over the quad of heroes so they weren't going to take any chances with this group of suspects.

There was more of them to deal with but authorities had to think of a way to get them to expose themselves because with the ban on the ice cream vendors how could they strike, somehow they had to convince their commanders to lift the ban for the sake of closing the case, hopefully this time for good. So while surveillance was still in full force the ban was eventually lifted and the ice cream vendors went back to work which led to the suspects jumping into action. Early one morning as detectives watched the men occupants of the house went riding to another part of the city, a neighborhood not nearly as well kept as theirs, stopping down the street from a house where a ice cream vendor was preparing his truck for the day's activities, detectives watched as the car driven by the suspects slowly advanced toward the house in question and learning from past experience backup had already been called, so it wasn't long before multiple police vehicles had the suspects car surrounded demanding that they exit it with their hands in the air, but the occupants remained put, so the order was repeated but this time with the added warning of being fired upon if instructions were not followed, but still there was no movement in the vehicle and by this time the swat team had arrived directing their heat seeking scopes straight at the suspects car, but to all of their surprise the scopes registered nothing, it was as if there was no one in the vehicle, but that couldn't be possible because they were looking at four people, two in the front and two in the back so how could they not be producing heat after all life is energy and energy of course has some heat elements otherwise the whole law of physics would have to be reevaluated. So authorities sought permission to converge on the vehicle and end this madness, then once orders were given they preceded with caution in light of the previous explosions, dynamite detecting dogs were employed so it would give them some idea of what they were up against but once the dogs returned detecting nothing, authorities converged in full force upon the vehicle of the four suspects, then as they approached the four men the suspects looked at them and began to laugh hysterically as if they considered them a joke, the detectives after seeing this began bursting the windows out of the car and then forcing the doors open because now they were furious and was about to show these men that this was no laughing matter. So they reached inside to pull the suspects out to arrest them but although they were plainly visible, they were not touchable, of course police figured this had to be some sort of trick so they reached in again and again their hands came out empty,'are you believing this'said one detective'I have to'another one said'are you going to call this in'one of them ask'we have a full squad here and all of us are witnessing the same thing so we know this is not an illusion, but my question is how is this possible' the four suspects were laughing so hard that one of the detectives just completely lost his temper and started firing his weapon into the car they occupied, once the bullets began flying the laughter suddenly stopped and was replaced with anger, anger so intense that the car began trembling with the suspects fury, and what happened next was so gruesome that even to this day it's still hard to understand, the explosion leveled everything within a five mile radius, no one or nothing was left standing, everyone that heard it will tell you that it sounded like the end of the world had come, which it had for a lot of people, but they will also tell you that no remains of the four men were ever found either and that puzzled investigators more than any other part of the mystery because some remains of everyone else had been accounted for. For some reason those four men who possess no energy for the heat seeking scopes to detect, or matter for the officers to grasp had just seem to have vanished without a trace, and what about the dynamite, how can explosive material not be detected by the best k-nine noses on the force, this was way out of these investigators league so they sought help from scientist, someone, anyone who could shed some sort of light as to how something like that could have taken place. Are their new laws in physics that need to be revealed or is there something that goes beyond science into another realm, a realm that's always been suppressed, things like this have been spoken of, but come on, really let's keep this real, it couldn't be, it just couldn't, but if not what happened that day, how can it be explained from a logical viewpoint, the truth is it can't, from all indications two realities clashed that day, man's logical view met the it can't be point of view, believe or not sometimes those two worlds do interlap and for lack of any real explanation somethings just get dismissed or labeled national security, I am very curious as to how an event known to the world as one of the most tragic unexplained mysteries ever recorded can suddenly be labeled top secret and to add to the mystery about a month later August ninth as a matter of fact another scorcher of a day that shattered previous heat records another explosion took place, yes from an ice cream vendor's truck and the irony of it all was that the truck had no legal rights to be on the street, but the part that triumph all else was that according to recorded video that was somehow revised from the rubble the same four men was responsible, impossible right, but the video was proven authentic, yea I know right, how could those same men that set off the first explosion have survived such a devastating atrocity and then cause another one a month later, well let's read on, by the time investigators secured and put all of the pieces together it was estimated that about twenty five thousand people died in that last explosion and the property value lost was in the billions, yet authorities were still clueless as to how to stop the ice cream vendor's murders, and now with local, state, and federal authorities seemingly at the mercy of the four unknown killers the public's outcry was loud and demanding. The world was at their mercy and the main question was when, where, and how many people would die in their next attack, so investigators went back to the house where the multiple families dwell hoping to find some kind of evidence as to how these missions were being carried out, they not only attain search warrants for that residence, but for the residence of the first two killers as well, then the two estates were searched inch by inch, top to bottom, the attics, the basements, furniture was dismantled, walls were leveled, the grounds were dug up in multiple areas, no place was left unexplored, but still no evidence was found. Then the next step was to attain search warrants for any property owned by any member of the two estates, the search was relentless and very thorough but still not one clue was found that explained how those four seemingly supernatural murderers was operating, frustration set in because no one wanted to believe that these bombs were being executed by ghosts or spirits, that just can't happen in this quote, unquote real world, but what other explanation could there be. A meeting was planned with mandatory attendance by all levels of crime solving agencies, the concept was unacceptable so now with the top crime fighters on the planet involved this case had to be solved and quickly because summer was about to end and no one wanted this case to go cold'this meeting will come to order'said special agent Stern'you all know why we're here and why it is of the most urgency that these murders be solved immediately, we've all examined the evidence so the floor is open on ideas as to how to bring this case to a close, then special agent Wilson replied'I'm thinking that somehow even though I haven't figured the exacts that these four killers are images or holograms of a mastermind with the financial independence to execute such a plan'then Stern said'that idea has merit, but what would be his motive'Wilson continued'I've given that some thought as well, what if the perpetrator had a terrifying experience either as a child or an adult by a ice cream vendor, maybe abuse in some form or another and now with vengeance in control plus the means to act upon it, he takes it out on all of them and the innocent customers are just expendable'. Silence came over the whole meeting with everyone carefully considering what special agent Wilson had just said and after extensive deliberations the concept started to make sense to all of them, in fact it was the only idea introduced in the meeting that put any real logic to how those four men could have survived such a explosion of that magnitude. So with the majority in agreement the main focus became known and unknown people with the skills and means of carrying out such a devious plan, the database revealed more of them than expected, now it was time to dig into the past of these newly formed suspects and see if any documented abuse involving an ice cream vendor truck driver had taken place, investigators had broken a very important rule in trying to solve this case, they had put all of their eggs in one basket so to speak, it was like solve or bust, but after circulating the names of the suspects it looked like it was all going to pay off. One of them stuck out like a sore thumb, his name was Raymond Robinson, his parents had divorced when he was seven years old, his mother had tried her best to raise him and his two sisters alone but without the help of child support because of their deadbeat dad she soon had to seek financial help to keep up with their needs and the support came from the neighborhood ice cream vendor. Raymond excelled above and beyond in technology, it was his motivation all the way through school and ended up earning him a scholarship to a prestige college where he graduated with honors, but after his mom started dating the ice cream vendor the abuse began soon after to him and his sisters, his mother could do very little to stop it because she was being abused as well. Then as the years passed at age fourteen, one of his sisters ran away from home and was found raped and murdered a month later, Raymond who was twelve at the time buried himself in his studies with a plan of destruction already brewing in his mind, then he came home one day and found his stepdad, the ice cream vendor raping his now only sister at age eleven, he tried to help her but was knocked unconscious by the abuser, when their mother got home the two of them told her about the rape but of course he denied the accusations, then violently attacked their mother with such force that she had to be hospitalized and later died from her wounds. Then with their mother deceased the two of them became wards of the state and because of their age no one wanted to adopt, but none of that even fazed Raymond's determination and after graduating college he applied for jobs that gave him access to the technology he needed and before long he mastered all areas of advance mechanisms, then those skills along with the pure hatred he had built for ice cream vendor truck drivers over the years led to a very destructive deadly combination, all of the investigators summarized that this had to be their man. Now if they were going to stop him before he killed again their plan had to be nearly perfect, so they looked up his address and surveillance was set up around the clock and by the zip code registered to his name authorities knew he lived among the elite, but to their surprise he was the elite of the elite, his mansion covered the entire block on which it sat with twenty four hour security, cameras everywhere, chauffeured driven limousine with all of the normalities swimming pools inside and out, tennis courts, bowling alleys, movie theaters, and then there was the helicopters, not to mention the jet, the plane, and the yacht, yes Mr. Robinson had everything money could buy but of all the luxuries in his possession his most valued prize was his laboratory where he spent most of his time, he never married, had no children in fact except for his staff he was a committed loner, then there was his sister Grace, his only remaining relative.

Grace was in a similar mode because of the traumatic experience she suffered when the ice cream vendor raped her as a child and then to top it off she felt totally guilty for her mother's death and that is the main reason that she never married or wanted children she just to put it plainly didn't trust men in general, in fact to some extent she feared them, she and her brother had been everything to each other since their mother was murdered by their stepdad. Grace hadn't excelled in school to the degree of her brother Raymond but she had exceptional knowledge, studying and mastering all levels of the law, vowing to put away all abusers without remorse, she devoted her life to not letting anyone suffer the same fate that her family had and as district attorney she found delight in every guilty verdicts but especially the abusers. So here they were brother and sister, survivors each one with a mission developed because of their tragic past and each one just as determine as the other to fulfill their perspective goal, with Grace angle seeking out justice while Raymond's was unsustainable, empathy goes out to his reasonings but a lot of innocent people were being murdered in the process, so in short he had to be stopped. Authorities couldn't legally get a search warrant for his property based on what they had for evidence and as long as ice cream vendors trucks were banned from residences it wasn't likely that he was going to strike again, so with summer coming to an end the decision was made that the ban had to be lifted even with the highest possible risk the ice cream trucks had to be allowed to roam the streets, but before that order was executed an implausible plan had to be devised and implemented and at all cost mistakes was not an option because Raymond was too smart and powerful to allow any loose ends. So another meeting was held with some recommending appealing to Grace, thinking that since she was one of them she would surely convince her brother to stop the madness and turn himself in while others argued that even though she was the district attorney her loyalty to her brother would supercede any other and that would lead to her warning him, destroying their case. The debate went on for hours with neither side convincing the other and then out of plain exhaust the meeting ended with no decision being made toward his sisters part in the plan but everyone conceded that the ban would be lifted and an army would be used if needed to bring this killer to justice, the news traveled the airwaves immediately being the top story of the day stating that the ice cream trucks would be riding again, the public demanded an explanation and one was given at a news conference set up by the F.B.I. with all cameras focused on him special agent Stevenson began'a person of interest has been arrested in this case and we feel very strongly that we have the right person and the danger is over, so we have decided to lift the ban allowing everyone to enjoy the remaining days left in this summer'then after completing that statement he declined to answer anymore questions. Now the pressure was on investigators to figure out how Raymond was placing those four hologram killers in a dynamite rigged vehicle and wiping out ice cream vendors trucks across the nation, they figured the only real chance they had would be to get into his laboratory, so they had a D.A. petitioning a judge on a constant level hoping to find at least one that would bend the rules a little for the sake of justice, all the while keeping this knowledge from the D.A.'s best Grace, Raymond's sister. It definitely was no easy task because of her devotion to her job she was in on just about every case in some form or another, so it didn't take her long to find out about this one but once she heard that her brother was the main suspect in the ice cream vendor murders it was like a light came on in her head, memories of her childhood started rushing through her mind, she recalled the big truck, the rape, her mother's death, her sister running away only to end up raped and murdered, her brother's constant beatings at the hands of the monster behind it all, their stepdad the ice cream vendor truck driver, yes it all made sense to her now, through the years she and her brother shared everything, there were no secrets until lately when his work in his laboratory took precedence over their impenetrable relationship, now that she thought about it her brother had been very secretive lately, sharing very little from his scientific work, only enough to keep her at bay. Then chills began running through her spine, that monster had turned her otherwise very meek, very humble brother into an even bigger monster, when she thought of all of those innocent people being murdered that had nothing to do with their uncanny abuse it sickened her, in fact her lunch came back up the same route it went down, she felt very faint, reality had set in, the thought rushed through her mind like a tidal wave, their going to kill my brother,'no'she heard herself say, then began screaming very loudly, the thought of life without her brother was overwhelming, he was all she had since their mother's death so many years ago, she couldn't allow that to happen, she had to somehow save her brother's life even though she fully agreed that he should pay for all of those innocent murders, she reasoned that if a jury of his peers heard the extenuating circumstances that led to his insane need for vengeance that they would somehow spare his life and just keep him locked up until death. So she went to the powers that be and agreed to lead the quest of her brother's capture, giving them permission to search the estate because of her residency there the search warrant would be legal and binding, she just wanted her brother's life spared in return, this was the break authorities had been seeking, although none of them favored taking the death penalty out of the equation, pressure dictated that they take the deal, at least the killer would be in a place where he could never harm anyone else. So a search warrant was issued but suppressed until Grace could get her brother out of the estate and that didn't take long to accomplish because Raymond trusted her without question, so that night Grace persuaded Raymond to go out with her to celebrate a major victory that she achieved that day in court, and of course her brother knowing how much that meant to his sister went eagerly, he had always supported his sister, the fact is that even though Raymond had become a monster himself he still enjoyed hearing of evildoers being put away because the pain was so real that even now as an adult he could feel the agony, but somehow he separated his mission from the crimes of the world, he had justified his plight in his mind as unavoidable, it didn't matter to him who get hurt in the process all ice cream vendors must be destroyed, and of course that logic was pure madness, but that was his reasoning, that was his pain. While he and his sister was out celebrating the search warrant was executed and not a moment too soon because police figured that since the news of the ice cream vendors trucks being able to resume operations was well known that this night was the calm before the storm and all indicators pointed toward Raymond Robinson making the headlines sometime the next day in tragic deed form, but now with access to his laboratory the authorities had no plans of letting that happen. Even after entering his mad lab investigators was at a loss as to understanding the high tech machines displayed around them so special experts were called in with hope of connecting something in the lab to the crimes that had taken place because everything they had to this point was all circumstantial and there was no way it would stand up in court, especially against a man with the wealth and power that Raymond had, his lawyers would chew them up and spit them out, they needed so much more and one of the members of the special task force may have given them just that. A row of machines in the rear of the rest held the technology needed to form self made holograms and though more research would have to be done to verify the discovery it was all authorities needed to make an arrest, so they moved quickly arresting him without incident as they was coming home, Raymond was in a good mood but that all changed as the handcuffs was being placed on him, his team of lawyers soon entered the courthouse asking for bail to release their employer, but due to the severity of the case bail was denied, but that didn't deter his high price lawyers who appealed that decision around the clock, news of the arrest was soon broadcast by every news media not only in the country but all over the globe, suspect captured in the ice cream vendor murders, it then went into detail as to who it was and how he was captured, and of course it became well known that he was the brother of a very popular D.A.,then as investigators continued their search of the lab, more and more evidence was found explaining how Raymond had pulled off all of those unspeakable crimes and didn't even have to be in the vicinity, it even became known that the first two killers who had died for the cause had been heavily indebted to Raymond and needless to say very loyal. After losing his friends, Raymond figured the price was too high, especially since he was a loner he didn't have many of them to begin with, so he devised a plan in which no one he cared about personally would get hurt and with his skills in high tech, holograms became the perfect answer, once locating his next target it then became a simple matter to set remote controlled vehicle to drive themselves to their appointed destination with the holograms intact, making the holograms obey his every command was also simple for someone with such an advanced mind, but planting the explosives in the vendor's trucks was another matter entirely, once the plan was in effect Raymond would monitor the surroundings for a while making sure nothing was amiss, then after he deemed everything clear hired explosive handlers would go to the scene, remove the dynamite from the car the holograms occupied and put it in it's perspective places on the truck, once placed it was set to go off at a certain time in the peak of the sweltering day, a time when it was estimated to due the most damage, genuous some would say, total madness say others, but whatever your viewpoint if not for an hunch by special agent Stevenson, that activity may have covered a much longer time frame, with countless of men, women, and children dying as a result. Raymond's trial was a mockery of the judicial system with news cameras covering every moment of it, it was a slam dunk for prosecutors with defense attorneys playing the insanity card, which after jurors heard the extenuating circumstances that led to his hatred of ice cream vendors, even if the death sentence hadn't been taken out of the equation, it wouldn't have been reality to expect all twelve jurors to agree on such a penalty, but they all did agree that he was too dangerous to ever be allowed to roam the world as a free man again and so life without the possibility of parole was the sentence placed on him, which of course angered a lot of the relatives of the murdered ones, not to mention some of the survivors that were marked for life because of him, but most of the public was satisfied with the verdict knowing he would never have a chance to hurt anyone again. Grace took it really hard knowing that for all intensive purposes her brother's life was over, but she did find joy in the fact that he was spared, she visits her brother daily trying to keep his spirit uplifted while the victims after completing the task of burying their dead tried to go on with their lives. Fall came, followed by Winter, and then Spring, these three season's interventions gave the public some time to heal, but as the days of Spring became shorter and shorter, the thought of summer became overwhelming in so many people's minds, thinking of the heated sticky days and of course the ice cream trucks running rapid, soon it would be business as usual with the cold multi colored delights soothing heated throats everywhere, but one thing is without doubt that no one will ever forget the summers of the mass murders. It's been thirty years since those tragic events took place which are now being told to a lot of people who wasn't around during that time, so to them it's a part of history known as the legend of the ice cream vendors murders. The End

I Must Prevail

written by Rocky Earl Smith

Trails bombarding my total existence, one two punches from life itself

The reason for it is outer suspense, leaving me feeling very inept

Though knocking me senseless I stand bold, looking the enemy in the eye

I must above all maintain control, life's obstacles are great I can't deny

When I can't move forward I'll stand firm, if knocked down I'll rise in place

There's vital things I have yet to learn, to remain competitive in this human race

I hear you can't keep a good man down, with patience wisdom and strength at my side

I'm bracing myself for the final round, because a positive reality I won't be denied

I, Fantasy

written by-Rocky Earl Smith\a.k.a. darkbrain

I soar from world to world just by thinking it, I stand victorious in every degree, I fly above the highest clouds just because, your thoughts are the pathway to my castle, I rule with exceptional grace, I am all powerful, I control your emotions, I control your actions, I blink and your life is in my domain, I snap my fingers and all of your wishes come true, in my world all things are possible, I am called Fantasy

The Rainbow Illusion

written by Rocky Earl Smith-a.k.a. Darkbrain

One day I was studying the different wonders in the sky and the detailed beauty overtook my senses, especially the rainbow the way the different colors came together to create the perfect portrait of grandeur, then my mind began looking over and beyond that rainbow. I didn't see a land called oz up there but I did see a place where dreams are born and dreams die, then as my mind looked pass that point I saw a area where all thoughts roam relaxed and totally free, my mind lit up with excitement as it entered the place where the conscious and subconscious met and focus on ideas to create a better existence between the two, and of course my mind had to stay awhile when it discovered that there was a perfect vacation site up there for my sanity.

I Am Vapor, Master of The Rainbow and Keeper of the Pot of Gold

written by Rocky Earl Smith-a.k.a. darkbrain

The rainbow is a symbol of absolute beauty and serenity, there are tales of a pot of gold at the end of each one of them which would seem possible considering the majestic aura they radiate, but that wasn't the case for the characters in this story, no their experience was anything but pleasant.'wow look at that rainbow'James shouted 'it is a beauty' Cynthia said'I wonder if we followed it would we find that famous pot of gold'James said without much thought'I doubt it besides you know that's just an old wives tale'Cynthia said without any thought'I know but with our bills the thought just crossed my mind'James said as the two of them just stood and gazed at the magnificent shades of colors, each of them in their own fantasy. While in a different part of the city another couple stood looking at the rainbow as well'you think if we followed it we'll find that pot of gold?' Cherry ask'get real, even if there was a pot of gold with our luck someone would get there just ahead of us and rub our nose in it'Zack said half jokingly and half depressed thinking of how handy that amount of money would be about this time'yea you're right but I can't help thinking of the life that kind of money would lead too, oh well back to reality, I guess I'll start dinner'Cherry said as she turned toward their small but modest home looking at it in disgust after coming out of her little fantasy.

Then she was stopped abruptly by Zack's voice as she heard him shout out with unbelievable excitement,'Cherry look, tell me I'm not imagining this, that rainbow looks like it ends in that bunch of trees over there','it sure does or I'm imagining it too'Cherry said barely able to contain herself and then for a moment they both just stood there neither of them wanting to even blink for fear that it would all be an illusion, then Zack not being able to withstand it any longer said'let's go and see'so they slowly started walking toward the trees, neither really believing they would find a pot of gold but hoping like crazy that it would be there. Once the neared the trees the anticipation brought on overwhelming anxiety, but as they entered the area of the heavily populated trees sure enough the rainbow ended but instead of finding the gold they saw a garden paradise with everything grown to perfection, it was like being in a very pleasant dream'Zack do you see what I see?'Cherry ask'I think so'Zack said as he took her by the hand and led her through this newly found promise land'let's see where it leads',the further they walked the more awesome the garden became until the next site immobilized them both as they stood there in total disbelief, Cherry's legs buckled as she fell to her knees weakened by the sheer glow of insurmountable gold and for a moment Zack was completely unaware that his wife was no longer standing by his side, the pot of gold displayed in front of them was mesmerizing to the point of overwhelming awe, their first inclination was not to move for fear of waking and finding it was all a dream, but after a little while longer they decided to go for it. Cherry was on her feet in an instant and ran as fast as her legs would take her toward that giant shining vision of security, but Zack had reached the pile already and was busy stuffing his pockets until the shining nuggets began to fall to the ground of the garden paradise, for a brief moment he didn't realize that all of them was full, Cherry's pockets didn't take as long to fill so now frustration began to set in, both of them had stuffed all the gold coins they could on their persons and it didn't even make a dent in this giant glowing mega bank, they looked around the garden trying to spot something that would hold a lot more of the treasure than they could possible hope to with their pockets alone, of course they were not planning on leaving any of it behind, they fully intended on returning to claim it all, but just in case the unthinkable happen and it wasn't there when they did come back for it they wanted to take as much with them as possible. They were so wrapped up in their thoughts of unspeakable riches that neither of them noticed the large figure that had appeared behind them'you're violating my gold 'said the huge form, the couple turned to see who was speaking even though neither one of them had any intentions on giving the money back, Zack was first to see the source of the voice and what he saw made him gasp with excitement. She was beautiful, right out of a fairy tale, her natural blonde hair flowed down her back, her buttocks, her long very shapely legs and stopped at her bare feet, her eyes were as red as fire itself, her face was sculptured out of pure beauty, then as his eyes followed the curves of her blemishless naked body observing every detail, he heard his mouth say'wow'then without realizing it he just stood there in an hypnotic trance.

Cherry was in a similar trance but from a different perspective, her eyes beheld another form right out of a fairy tale, he was tall and bulging with masculinity, his face was sculptured in the aura of royalty, his body was built like a Greek God and as she stared deep into his fiery red eyes her mind was overcome with an unquenchable desire that consumed her whole body, then he smiled at her and it was as if nothing or no one else existed and said'you are the one I've been waiting for, come and share a world with me that goes beyond your wildest dreams'immediately Cherry began walking toward him while Zack's vision of perfection had offered him a similar life with her fiery eyes melting away any inhibitions as she said to him'my gold is guarded by this garden and will release it only after I have found a suitable mate, help me free my treasure and I will be yours forever'her words were as soft and enticing as a magic melody and without hesitation Zack began walking toward her, then as Zack and Cherry approached the huge figure they became aware of one the other presence'kill her'Zack's vision told him and he grab Cherry by the neck and squeezed until her life exited her body, then threw her limp body aside like garbage, the huge figure then released his mind and slowly reality set in. The garden paradise was actually shrub, the pot of gold was just an old waterless well, but the murder of his wife was real, Cherry's body lay in the midst of the shrub with it's eyes bulging out from being choked to death and as Zack stood there in disbelief the whole illusion had disappeared, the huge figure, the rainbow, and the pot of gold, it had been awhile since the rain had stopped so people were moving around so spotting Zack still in a state of shock looking down at his murdered wife's body didn't take long, after first responders were called to the scene Cherry was officially pronounced dead, Zack didn't even try to deny he had done it but when he was ask about a motive there was no answer, he figured who would believe him anyway, in fact as he thought back on the event he wasn't sure it had happened himself. As time passed there were a few rainy days but no rainbow, that is until one day right before Easter, it wasn't a thunderstorm but it was hard and steady and continued the whole day and night bringing in Easter Sunday at which it stopped. That morning the air was so fresh it cleared any blockage in the lungs, the day gave out a radiance that seemed to give a glow to everything and right there in the center of the sky was that majestic multi colored rainbow stretching across the heavens like a bridge to some mysterious paradise, the site was so spellbinding that crowds had gathered to watch it's magnificent beauty'will you look at that'Marcia pointed out'I've never seen it look so elegant','it does look awesome'Katrina added as the two of them continued to stare at the heavenly wonder, then Marcia stated'I could stand here all day just admiring it but I guess we should get ready for church','yea I can't wait to show off my new dress'Katrina added as they were turning to go into their home, after Marcia had entered Katrina followed but turned to get one more glimpse of the rainbow before closing the door'Marcia'Katrina called out,'What is it?'Marcia asked,'the rainbow, it appears to end in that vacant field across the street'Katrina said puzzlingly,'don't be ridiculous'Marcia told her,'no seriously look',Katrina insisted, so Marcia turned to look and sure enough the rainbow seem to bend right out of the sky into the vacant field across the street from their house,'I don't believe it'Marcia said astonished, the two of them were so fixated on the unheard of miracle that they hadn't noticed the neighborhood crowd that had gathered with some heading toward the vacant field while others had taken out their cell phones and were recording the entire event and still others were calling everyone they knew spreading the news like wildfire, and still others were reluctant to take any type of action thinking that this had to be some kind of publicity stunt. Marcia and Katrina were a part of the onlookers heading toward the vacant field with their cell phone cameras in hand, no one knowing what to expect but all doubting that a pot of gold would be there, but as the crowd drew closer to the field their whole attitude changed as they beheld a shining huge glowing pot filled with gold nuggets, at first they all looked in bewilderment and then it started to dawn on some and then others that even though this could be just a magical dream it looked real enough to touch, and touch them they would as some and then others began to make a mad dash for those glowing treasured coins and it didn't take long before the situation got completely out of hand, as each one rushed to claim all the money that was possible, greed reared it dangerous head which in turn gave anger an opening into the event, and of course once anger arrived on the scene, tragedy soon followed in the form of deadly deeds and acts. Loud explosive sounds echoed through the air but the crowd remained intact, very few of them noticed that some of their neighbors were falling to the ground in a dead state and even fewer of them cared, then the number of people being killed escalated to the point where it couldn't be ignored, although it still barely slowed the aggressive behavior displayed by the once peaceful law abiding citizens that saw this gold as the answer to all of their problems, then there were only a few of them left but the killings continued because no one wanted to share, now an eerie silence flowed across the once lively neighborhood, with the huge figure standing in the midst of it, just like it began it ended, so he took his pot of gold and his rainbow then vanished, no one could explain how such logical respectful neighbors had become violent degenerates, no there was just no apparent reason for the insanity of how this glorious day set aside to celebrate the Lord's victory over the grave had sent so many to their's, the church would have a lot of vacant seats in their services today with all the new suits and dresses remaining in their perspective places, the vacant field was now a memorial, that Easter Sunday would stay in the headlines for a long time to come

Spring was in full bloom, nature took extra care of all of it's life recreations, but substance was needed to fully capture the essence of pure beauty, so nature brought forth rain, lots and lots of rain and of course with that amount of moisture falling from the clouds the appearance of the rainbow was inevitable, and on one day in the month of May it was there, looking like an array of angels spreading across the heavens forming a perfect arc, it looked so amazing that people gathered from miles around to behold this awesome view, one whole crew of construction workers just stopped working to gaze at it's form, another crew took an early break including the boss, no one wanted to miss this vision of perfection, it was like everyone was seeing it for the first time. While the city's population was mesmerized with the latest hypnotic view in the sky the huge figure appeared in the midst of them with the mindset of testing all that gazed upon the rainbow, not just a specific area, with all the rain that had fallen lately the huge figure felt more powerful than ever so he decided to expand his experiment, he had designated the spot of his rainbow's end base on the direction of the crowds that had gathered, but now as he looked around this enormous crowd was focus in multiple direction so he had no idea how this experiment would work but with all of the extra power oozing from his person he felt he could accomplish anything, and this challenge actually gave him motivation because he had become bored with the previous small events, so taking his deceits to higher extremities was just what the doctor ordered. The whole city was under the illusion of grandeur, the huge figure had directed his rainbow to multiple delusions, having everyone thinking they were about to be rich beyond their wildest dreams and of course this brought on mass confusion, which in turn brought on mass greed and mass greed never produce a happy ending, now the whole city lay in ruins, there were fires, there were snipers, vehicular manslaughters, naturally good people became murderers showing no sign of remorse, the sight of that much gold had corrupted even the purest of hearts, the thought of totally independent wealth brainwashed those people to the degree of sinister evil which left no one safe, neither family members or friends were exempt, the death angel worked overtime and when all the commotion stopped, no one in the city stood without some type of ailment they had receive during the onslaught, the huge figure looked at his triumphant deed and felt good about himself, his confidence grew to an all time high, he felt his will was supreme and looking around at his handy work he had no reason to think otherwise, but he realized that he had used the bulk of his energy for the time being so he would wait on more power and his next appearance will be one for the record books and then he was gone taking his rainbow as well as his gold with him. By now the news of the destruction was well known, but no one had a clue as to who or what had implemented it and that fact alone sent widespread fear throughout the hemisphere, people were afraid to come out of their homes because as far as they knew for some unknown reason otherwise prominent level headed neighbors was killing one another, so being leery of their friends and neighbors was an understatement, trust became a thing of the past and for a very good reason, nothing made sense anymore, security was on twenty four hour alert, people that could afford video cameras had them placed in every direction and everyone exercised their second amendment right, but nothing major happened, soon even though the public was still uneasy the fear subsided, some even began to think it was just an isolated incident. The spring season was coming to an end, but for some reason the rain began coming out of the clouds in an overflow, on one occasion it would rain everyday and night for a week straight and since the rain was a power source for the huge figure it wouldn't be long before the rainbow appeared in the sky and the more powerful the huge figure becomes the more radiant the rainbow would look and the larger the pot of gold would be, then as if on cue about noon one day in June it appeared, looking at it said it all, the huge figure had outdone himself, the site of this rainbow left everyone speechless, it was perfect, combined with the fresh air, blue skies and soothing temperatures this day brought good vibes to all who beheld it, there were smiles on everyone's face, outdoor plans were made in bulk, people greeted others with handshakes and hugs, the aura of happiness overtook everyone, pleasant thoughts, good deeds was a part of the norm, as it looked nothing or nobody could even come close to spoiling this gloriously magnificent moment in time, at least that's what the huge figure wanted everyone to believe, because the event he had in mind would be just as tragic as this illusion of perfection consuming all thoughts at this moment, and it was going to hit these people like a ton of bricks. There was a special festival in celebration of the state's passing of the gambling law, this law had been out voted time and time again, but now by the smallest of margins it passed and the party was on, the huge figure saw the idea situation, gambling money, hmm this state just passed laws legalizing gambling and I have enough money to send everyone involved into chaos, this will be my finest work to date, then without delay the huge figure directed his rainbow's end right in the midst of the festival, and needless to say it took everyone by surprise, suddenly the largest celebration in the state became the quietest place in the state, I mean seriously you could hear a pin drop, people jaws hung open, their movements immobilized, no one could believe what they was looking at, but there it was right in the center of them all, the largest, glowing pot of gold nuggets and coins that any of them could have even fantasize, and it seem to stretch as high as the rainbow itself, yes the huge figure had truly outdone himself.

As he looked over the thousands of celebrators standing in awe of his magic the huge figure noticed a few of them had gathered together with gleams in their eyes, idealistic motives no doubt, so he concentrated his listening super ability toward their conversation'I tell you all, if we don't take advantage of this gift we're not the leaders we claim to be, look at them they're as confused as lost pets, but once they put their head around this nothing will stop them'Jim told his fellow casino owners and statesman 'brilliant idea Jim but how do we convince literary half the state that this is just a publicity stunt, some of them are bound to realize that that gold is real and once that's been established even the dumbest of them will know that all of our fortunes combined wouldn't produce that amount of money'Sam stated'that's the reason we can't waste anymore time, if my idea doesn't work then we've lost nothing, but if it does, we'll own the country'Jim said with pride as he took control of the situation'ladies and gentlemen the site you're seeing represents the fortune you can win when you visit one or all of the four casinos we've built conveniently for the citizens of our great state, no matter which direction you take north, south, east or west, there's a chance to win enough money to live like royalty, so enjoy this our grand opening celebration and remember the possibilities are endless once you enter the doors of our casinos'then Jim looked the crowd over hoping his speech had the effect desired and sure enough a good portion of the party goers had hinge on his every word, but others including his fellow business partners were in a hypnotic trance, you see the huge figure had heard everything, the before and after remarks and went to work immediately to thwart those deceptive ideas by adding more gold to the pot, pure unblemished nuggets and coins stood like a shining tower that reached into the heavens, at this point the situation became hopeless, all of the celebrators weren't business oriented, but all of them did exercise their common sense which dictated that no human could produce this amount of riches, so once the gold was authenticated the rush was on. It became a hideous site, thankfully the news crews subcuum to the incredible illusion as well or the catastrophe would have been viewed live by the entire world, men, women, and children were trampled to death, fights ensued and killings followed, the statesmen, the casino owners and everyone that worked for them had become victims as well, yes greed had triumph again, this time on a much larger scale and still no one had a clue as to why such a joyous occasion became the deadliest day in the state's history because the huge figure had disappeared without a trace and of course he took his rainbow and pot of gold with him. Because of the mega number of citizens that perished that day it upset the whole economic value, every level of government was affected, the casino law previously passed was immediately repealed and the site that had been chosen to hold the grand opening celebration on became a memorial that would make sure that that bill never became a law in that state again, meanwhile the huge figure was constantly learning the key principles of what made man tick and vowed that his next appearance would make all else fail in comparison. Time passed and summer was in full effect so there wasn't a lot of rainy days in the forecast, that is until the fourth of July approached, it was like nature had decided to join forces with the huge figure because rain became a norm as this country's independence day neared, and of course the more it rain the more powerful that mysterious figure became, then the night before that celebrated day it seem like every cloud in the sky dumped it's entire load on the earth and when dawn appeared so did that heavenly multi colored arc, since the huge figure wanted to make this appearance his legacy he chose the location carefully, a area that would get the whole world's attention in a first class manner, the residence of the most powerful man in the world, the White House, so the stage was set as many residents of Washington D.C. looked into the sky totally mesmerize by the glowing wonder stretched across it, then as more and more felt compelled to gaze into the magical colors the arc suddenly seem to end right in the backgrounds of the most famous estate on the planet, and now the secured icon was the main focus point of all the residents and visitors alike, of course the secret service was all over the situation, but this was like no other security breach any of them had ever faced, and as the huge figure had anticipated it got the world's attention very quickly because the news media was on it too, the site was so awesome that even the White House staff had stopped their regular duties and come out to see the giant shining pot filled with more money than the treasury department, luckily the President and first family were on vacation, but was kept inform of the predicament, and then as the world looked on the huge figure magically multiplied the treasure to divine status, and then as if that wasn't enough another pot of equal proportion appeared next to it on the left and then one of the same value appeared on the right, in essence there was so much gold on the backgrounds of the fame estate that the sun's light was no match for the brilliant glider, the huge figure was elated, his power was so great this time that it was all he could do to stop at this point, now it was showtime with his magic at the helm the stage was set as he cast his hypnotic vibes into the atmosphere, they then slowly descended upon all who viewed the enormous fortress of glowing treasure and the rush was on

The huge figure had witnessed greed bring nothing but destruction among the lesser of these class of entities now he would see if the elite had the some response, since the illusion had began every level of government security had been alerted and ready to respond, the secret service had increased their personnel, the department of homeland security were on the grounds, along with the F.B.I. and the C.I.A., the secretary of defense was keeping the Pentagon up to date, every precaution had been taken because this was a situation no one could quite figure out, but all considered it to be a threat to national security. Then when the rush began things quickly took a turn for the worst as thousands of people lost all touch with reality, thinking why should the rich claim it all when they needed it much more and they would stop at nothing to get as much of that precious treasure as they could, once the powers that be saw the mad look in the eyes of the mob they know that talking to them would do little to no good so immediately the military armed forces was dispatched and the war began. The thousands of crazed people already on hand were joined by thousands of more and the numbers kept increasing as time went on, the three giant pots of solid gold which people could see from around the globe via satellite, had completely rob sanity from the minds of all so anyone who was capable of getting there got there with one purpose in their head, to get rich quick. Martial Law was declared and all people were ordered all the streets, not that anyone listen they were like mindless zombies and the pots of gold possess each of their brains, so non lethal tactics were implemented to slow down the onslaught, tear gas, rubber bullets, K-nines, every form of defense whose purpose was to spare lives, but none of them had any real effect there was just too many of them and the multitude of deranged financial independence seekers began to take control. The officials in power saw the situation becoming dire so the order was given to restore peace, regardless of the way it had to be done, the armed forces already in formation was ordered to ready their weapons, orders were given again for the mob to disperse, but they fell on deaf ears, the noise was so great that no news reporters could broadcast from the ground and actually had trouble hearing from the air, then with no other recourse orders were given to fire and fire they did, bodies were already blanketing the grounds, now they began to stack with precision and with people firing back, the military suffered a great amount of casualties as well, there was war among the mob, war between the mob and the military, with the news cameras on the helicopters recording the entire battle, the war seem to be an endless one because as fast as some fell others were arriving, but it was becoming an huge effort to get near the gold because of all the corpses creating great walls, then some began to find different purposes for the dead bodies, shields, stacking them on top of one another creating corpse ladders trying to climb high enough to start confiscating the treasures from the pots of gold, but about then a deafening boom was heard and then there was silence, the smoke was so thick that it blocked the rays from the sun and breathing in this mess was not an option, the world didn't get to see what took place after the bomb exploded because there was no news coverage of it, the helicopter that had been handling the only remaining view to the media had succumb to the explosion. No one was allowed to enter the Washington D.C. area until the smoke cleared and when it did vanish the District of Columbia was completely leveled, nothing moved within it's city limits, no people, no animals, there were no fowl flying in the air above it, not even the insects had survived, but as planes and helicopters view the remnant, one of their first thoughts is to see what kind of damage the bomb had had on the source of the confusion, the three large pots of gold, but needless to say the huge figure had already taken his gold and rainbow and disappeared, none of the polished treasure remained, not physically anyway, but it would always be there in everyone's memory, a memory that will haunt all who saw that uncanny battle for the rest of their lives. The huge figure marveled at how the power of greed totally dominated these primitive creatures, now realizing that this planet could be rendered helpless by their lust, the huge figure had visited a great number of worlds, some with creatures even more primitive than these, but never had he witnessed a more savage existence between the inhabitants, and although he know complete domination could be attained through the illusion of financial independence, the thought of ruling this world brought unimaginable boredom to his thoughts, so he decided to seek entertainment in another realm, hopefully a more challenging reality, so he took his rainbow and his gold and exited the earth's atmosphere in search of amusement. Yes I know the huge figure's identity was never revealed, that is until he decided to leave, then and only then did he make his identity known in big letters made from rain clouds across the heavens that read [I am Vapor, master of the rainbow and keeper of the pot of gold and I shall return]

The end

True Freedom

written by\Rocky Earl Smith

Look at the stars, their brightness is unique, it's hard to believe they're so many light years away, it looks like I can just reach up and grab the one of my choice, at least it looks so attainable. It's within my sight but not my might, my mind can reach them but my body can't, this body is so limited it's like a burden with gravity in full control, yes gravity's in charge of my body but can't touch my mind, my spirit. My spirit travels the universe without boundaries, the freedom I experience is mindboggling, the rush is intoxicating, I'm so high at this moment on nothing but the natural stimulants that my mind produces, no feeling on earth can match the realness, the wholesome attributes that the spirit generates. When I leave this prison known as the body, then and only then will I truly be free

Printed in the United States
By Bookmasters